FALCONER

FALCONER

JOHN CHEEVER

ALFRED A. KNOPF / NEW YORK / 1977

THIS IS A BORZOI BOOK
PUBLISHED BY ALFRED A. KNOPF, INC.
Copyright © 1975, 1977 by John Cheever
All rights reserved under International
and Pan-American Copyright Conventions.
Published in the United States
by Alfred A. Knopf, Inc., New York,
and simultaneously in Canada
by Random House of Canada Limited, Toronto.
Distributed by Random House, Inc., New York.

A portion of this book originally
appeared in Playboy magazine.

Library of Congress Cataloging in Publication Data
Cheever, John.   Falconer.
I. Title
PZ3.C3983Fal3   [PS3505.H6428]   76-19382
ISBN 0-394-48347-2
Manufactured in the United States of America
First Edition

To
FEDERICO CHEEVER

FALCONER

The main entrance to Falconer—the only entrance for convicts, their visitors and the staff—was crowned by an escutcheon representing Liberty, Justice and, between the two, the sovereign power of government. Liberty wore a mobcap and carried a pike. Government was the federal Eagle holding an olive branch and armed with hunting arrows. Justice was conventional; blinded, vaguely erotic in her clinging robes and armed with a headsman's sword. The bas-relief was bronze, but black these days—as black as unpolished anthracite or onyx. How many hundreds had passed under this, the last emblem most of them would see of

man's endeavor to interpret the mystery of imprisonment in terms of symbols. Hundreds, one guessed,
thousands, millions was close. Above the escutcheon
was a declension of the place-names: Falconer Jail
1871, Falconer Reformatory, Falconer Federal Peni-
tentiary, Falconer State Prison, Falconer Correctional
Facility, and the last, which had never caught on:
Daybreak House. Now cons were inmates, the assholes
were officers and the warden was a superintendent.
Fame is chancy, God knows, but Falconer—with its
limited accommodations for two thousand miscreants
—was as famous as Newgate. Gone was the water
torture, the striped suits, the lock step, the balls and
chains, and there was a softball field where the gallows
had stood, but at the time of which I'm writing, leg
irons were still used in Auburn. You could tell the men
from Auburn by the noise they made.

Farragut (fratricide, zip to ten, #734–508–32)
had been brought to this old iron place on a late summer's day. He wore no leg irons but was manacled to
nine other men, four of them black and all of them
younger than he. The windows of the van were so high
and unclean that he could not see the color of the sky
or any of the lights and shapes of the world he was
leaving. He had been given forty milligrams of methadone three hours earlier and, torpid, he wanted to see
the light of day. The driver, he noticed, stopped for
traffic lights, blew his horn and braked on steep hills,
but this was all they seemed to share with the rest of
humanity. The inestimable shyness of men seemed to
paralyze most of them, but not the man manacled to
his right. He was a gaunt man with bright hair and a

face hideously disfigured by boils and acne. "I hear they
have a ball team and if I can play ball I'll be all right.
Just so long as I can pitch a game I'll stay alive," he
said. "If I can play ball that'll be enough for me. I never
know the score, though. That's the way I pitch. The
year before last I pitched a no-hitter for North Edmons-
ton and I didn't know about it until I come off the
mound and heard everybody yelling. And I never got
laid free, never once. I paid anywhere from fifty cents
to fifty dollars, but I never once shot a lump for free. I
guess that's like not knowing the score. Nobody ever
give it to me willingly. I know hundreds of men, not so
good-looking as me, who get it for nothing all the time,
but I never got it once, not once for nothing. I just wish
I had it free, once."

The van stopped. The man on Farragut's left was
tall, and striding out of the van into the yard, threw
Farragut to his knees. Farragut got to his feet. He saw
the escutcheon for the first and, he thought, the last
time. This was where he would die. Then he saw the
blue sky and nailed his identity to it and to the phrasing
of four letters that he had begun to write to his wife,
his lawyer, his governor and his bishop. A handful of
people watched them quickstep across the yard. Then
he distinctly heard a voice say, "But they look so nice!"
That would have been some innocent, some stray, and
Farragut heard a man in uniform say, "Turn your back
and any one of them would put a shiv in it." But the
stray was right. The blue in the space between the van
and the prison was the first spread of blue some of
them had seen in months. How extraordinary it was
and how truly pure they seemed! They would never

again look so well. The light of the sky, shining into their condemned faces, showed a great richness of purpose and innocence. "They murder," said the guard, "they rape, they stuff babies into furnaces, they'd strangle their own mother for a stick of chewing gum." Then he turned from the stray to the convicts and began to call: "You're going to be good boys, you're gonna be good boys, you're gonna be good, good boys. . . ." He spread out his call like a train whistle, a hound's belling, some late-night lonely song or cry.

They pulled one another up some stairs into a shabby room. Falconer was very shabby, and the shabbiness of the place—everything one saw and touched and smelled had the dimension of neglect—gave the impression, briefly, that this must surely be the twilight and the dying of enforced penance, although there was a tenanted death house in the north of the place. The bars had been enameled white many years ago, but the enamel had been worn back to iron at the chest level, where men instinctively held them. In a farther room the guard who called them good boys unlocked their irons and the deep pleasure of being able to move his arms and his shoulders freely was something Farragut shared with the others. They all rubbed their wrists with their hands. "What time you got?" asked the man with boils. "Ten-fifteen," said Farragut. "I mean what time of year," said the man. "You got one of them calendar watches. I wanna know the time of year. Here, let me see it, let me see it." Farragut unstrapped his expensive watch and passed it to the stranger and the stranger put it in his pocket. "He stole my watch," Farragut said to the guard. "He just stole my watch."

"Oh, did he rahlly," said the guard, "did he rahlly steal your watch?" Then he turned to the thief and asked, "How long was your vacation?" "Ninety-three days," said the thief. "Is that the longest you been out?" "The time before last I was out for a year and a half," said the thief. "Will wonders never cease?" asked the guard. But all of this, all that there was to be seen and heard, was wasted on Farragut, who perceived nothing but paralysis and terror.

They were marshaled into a broken-down truck with wooden benches and driven down a road within the walls. At a turn in the road Farragut saw a man in prison grays feeding bread crusts to a dozen pigeons. This image had for him an extraordinary reality, a promise of saneness. The man was a convict and he and the bread and the pigeons were all unwanted but for reasons unknown to Farragut the image of a man sharing his crusts with birds had the resonance of great antiquity. He stood in the truck to watch for as long as he could. He was similarly moved when, in the building they entered, he saw, high on a water pipe at the ceiling, a tarnished silver Christmas garland. The irony was banal but it seemed, like the man feeding birds, to represent a grain of reason. Under the Christmas garland they went into a room furnished with writing chairs whose legs were broken, whose varnish was gone, whose writing surfaces were scarred with initials and obscenities and which seemed, like everything else in Falconer, to have been salvaged from some municipal dump. The first of the screenings was a psychological test that Farragut had already taken in the three drug addiction clinics that he had been confined to.

"Are you afraid of germs on doorknobs?" he read; "Would you like to hunt tigers in the jungle?" The irony of this was immeasurably less penetrating and moving than the man feeding birds and the silver link to Christmas, hung on a pipe. It took them half that day to answer the five hundred questions and then they were marshaled into the mess hall for a meal.

This was much older and larger than what he had seen in the house of detention. I-beams crossed the ceiling. In a tin pitcher on a window sill were some wax flowers whose colors, in that somber place, seemed fiery. He ate sour food with a tin spoon and dropped his spoon and plate into dirty water. Silence was enforced by the administration, but they had themselves enforced a segregation that put the blacks in the north, the whites in the south, with a middle ground for the men who spoke Spanish. After chow his physical, religious and professional characteristics were examined and then, after a long delay, he was led alone into a room where three men in cheap business suits were sitting at a wrecked desk. At either end of the desk were sheathed flags. On the left was a window in which he could see the blue sky beneath whose light he guessed a man might still be feeding pigeons. His head, neck and shoulders had begun to ache and he was very stooped by the time he reached this tribunal and felt himself to be a very small man, a runt, someone who had never experienced or tasted or imagined the greatness of immodesty.

"You are a professor," said the man on the left, who seemed to speak for the three. Farragut did not raise his head to see his face. "You are a professor and the education of the young—of all those who seek learning —is your vocation. We learn by experience, do we not, and as a professor, distinguished by the responsibilities of intellectual and moral leadership, you have chosen to commit the heinous crime of fratricide while under the influence of dangerous drugs. Aren't you ashamed?" "I want to be sure that I get my methadone," Farragut said. "Oh, is there no shame in you!" the man exclaimed. "We are here to help. We are here to help. Until you confess to shame you will have no place in the civilian world." Farragut made no reply. "Next," the man said, and Farragut was shown out a door at the back. "I'm Tiny," a man there said. "Hurry up. I ain't got all day."

Tiny's size was frightening. He was not tall, but his bulk was so unnatural that his clothes would have had to be sewn for him alone, and in spite of what he said about haste he walked very slowly, impeded by the bulk of his thighs. His gray hair was cut like a brush and you could see his scalp. "You got cellblock F," he said. "F stands for fucks, freaks, fools, fruits, first-timers, fatasses like me, phantoms, funnies, fanatics, feebies, fences and farts. There's more, but I forget it. The guy who made it up is dead." They went up a sloping tunnel past groups of men who hung around talking like men on the street. "F is temporary for you, I think," said Tiny. "The funny way you talk, they'll put you in A, where they have the lieutenant governor and the secretary of commerce and all the millionaires." Tiny turned right and he followed him through an open door into the cellblock. Like everything else, it was shabby, disorderly and malodorous, but his cell had a window and he went to this and saw some sky, two high water towers, the wall, more cellblocks and a corner of the yard that he had entered on his knees. His arrival in the block was hardly noticed. While he was making his bed, someone asked, "You rich?" "No," said Farragut. "You clean?" "No," said Farragut. "You suck?" "No," said Farragut. "You innocent?" Farragut didn't reply. Someone at the back of the block struck a guitar and began to sing in a tuneless bluegrass voice: "I got those innocence blues/I'm feeling blue all the time. . . ." This could barely be heard above the noise of radios which—talking, singing, performing music—sounded like any city street at closing time or later.

No one spoke to Farragut at all until, just before the lights went off, the man by whose voice he recognized the singer came to his door. He was skinny and old and had a light, unpleasant voice. "I'm Chicken Number Two," he said. "Don't go looking around for Chicken Number One. He's dead. You've probably read about me in the paper. I'm the famous tattooed man, the light-fingered second-story worker who spent his fortune on body art. I'll show you my pictures someday when I get to know you better." He leered. "But what I come to tell you is that it's all a mistake, a terrible mistake, I mean you being here. They won't find out tomorrow, it'll be a week or two before they discover this mistake they made, but when they discover it they'll be so sorry, so ashamed of themselves, they'll feel so guilty that the governor will kiss your ass on Fifth Avenue during the Christmas rush. Oh, they'll feel so sorry. Because you see, every trip we make, even for the boneheads, has something good at the end of it

like a pot of gold or a fountain of youth or an ocean or
a river nobody ain't never seen before or at least a big
porterhouse steak with a baked potato. There has to be
something good at the end of every journey and that's
why I wanted you to know that it's all a terrible mistake. And during the time you're waiting for them to
discover this big mistake you'll have your visitors. Oh, I
can tell, just by the way you sit there, that you got
thousands of friends and lovers and a wife, of course.
Your wife will come to visit you. She'll have to come
and visit you. She ain't going to be able to divorce you
unless you sign the papers and she'll have to bring
them here herself. So all I wanted to tell you is what
you already knew—it's all a big mistake, a terrible
mistake."

Farragut's first visitor was his wife. He was raking leaves in yard Y when the PA said that 734–508–32 had a visitor. He jogged up the road past the firehouse and into the tunnel. It was four flights up to cellblock F. "Visitor," he said to Walton, who let him into his cell. He kept his white shirt prepared for visits. It was dusty. He washed his face and combed his hair with water. "Don't take nuttin but a handkerchief," said the guard. "I know, I know, I know. . . ." Down he went to the door of the visitors' room, where he was frisked. Through the glass he saw that his visitor was Marcia.

There were no bars in the visitors' room, but the glass windows were chicken-wired and open only at the top. A skinny cat couldn't get in or out, but the sounds of the prison moved in freely on the breeze. She would, he knew, have passed three sets of bars—clang, clang, clang—and waited in an anteroom where there were pews or benches, soft-drink engines and a display of the convicts' art with prices stuck in the frames. None of the cons could paint, but you could always count on some wet-brain to buy a vase of roses or a marine sunset if he had been told that the artist was a lifer. There were no pictures on the walls of the visitors' room but there were four signs that said: NO SMOKING. NO WRITING. NO EXCHANGE OF OBJECTS. VISITORS ARE ALLOWED ONE KISS. These were also in Spanish. NO SMOKING had been scratched out. The visitors' room in Falconer, he had been told, was the most lenient in the East. There were no obstructions—nothing but a three-foot counter between the free and the unfree. While he was being frisked he looked around at the other visitors—not so much out of curiosity as to see if there was anything here that might offend Marcia. A con was holding a baby. A weeping old woman talked to a young man. Nearest to Marcia was a Chicano couple. The woman was beautiful and the man was caressing her bare arms.

Farragut stepped into this no man's land and came on hard, as if he had been catapulted into the visit by mere circumstance. "Hello darling," he exclaimed as he had exclaimed "Hello darling" at trains, boats, airports, the foot of the driveway, journey's end; but in the past he would have worked out a timetable, aimed at the soonest possible sexual consummation.

"Hello," she said. "You look well."

"Thank you. You look beautiful."

"I didn't tell you I was coming because it didn't seem necessary. When I called to make an appointment they told me you weren't going anywhere."

"That's true."

"I haven't been here sooner because I've been in Jamaica with Gussie."

"That sounds great. How's Gussie?"

"Fat. She's gotten terribly fat."

"Are you getting a divorce?"

"Not now. I don't feel like talking with any more lawyers at this point."

"Divorce is your prerogative."

"I know." She looked at the Chicano couple. The man had stroked his way up to the hair in the girl's armpits. Both their eyes were shut.

"What," she asked, "do you find to talk about with these people?"

"I don't see much of them," he said, "excepting at chow and we can't talk then. You see, I'm in cellblock F. It's sort of a forgotten place. Like Piranesi. Last Tuesday they forgot to spring us for supper."

"What is your cell like?"

"Twelve by seven," he said. "The only thing that belongs to me is the Miró print, the Descartes and a color photograph of you and Peter. It's an old one. I took it when we had a house on the Vineyard. How is Peter?"

"Fine."

"Will he ever come to see me?"

"I don't know, I really don't know. He doesn't ask for you. The social worker thinks that, for the general welfare, it's best at the moment that he not see his father in jail for murder."

"Could you bring me a photograph?"

"I could if I had one."

"Couldn't you take one?"

"You know I'm no good with a camera."

"Anyway, thank you for sending me the new watch, dear."

"You're welcome."

Someone on cellblock B struck a five-string banjo and began to sing: "I got those cellblock blues/I'm feeling blue all the time/I got those cellblock blues/ Fenced in by walls I can't climb. . . ." He was good. The voice and the banjo were loud, clear and true, and brought into that border country the fact that it was a late summer afternoon all over that part of the world. Out the window he could see some underwear and fatigues hung out to dry. They moved in the breeze as if this movement—like the movements of ants, bees and geese—had some polar ordination. For a moment he felt himself to be a man of the world, a world to which his responsiveness was marvelous and absurd. She opened her bag and looked for something. "The army must have been a good preparation for this experience," she said.

"Sort of," he said.

"I never understood why you so liked the army."

He heard, from the open space in front of the main

entrance, a guard shouting: "You're going to be good boys, aren't you? You're going to be good boys. You're going to be good, good, good boys." He heard the dragging ring of metal and guessed they'd come from Auburn.

"Oh, dammit," she said. Peevishness darkened her face. "Oh, Goddammit," she said with pure indignation.

"What's wrong?" he asked.

"I can't find my Kleenex," she said. She was foraging in the bag.

"I'm sorry," he said.

"Everything seems to fight me today," she said, "absolutely everything." She dumped the contents of her bag onto the counter.

"Lady, lady," said the turnkey, who sat above them on an elevated chair like a lifeguard. "Lady, you ain't allowed to have nothing on the counter but soft drinks and butt cans."

"I," she said, "am a taxpayer. I help to support this place. It costs me more to keep my husband in here than it costs me to send my son to a good school."

"Lady, lady, please," he said. "Get that stuff off the counter or I'll have to kick you out."

She found the small box of paper and pushed the contents of her handbag back to where they belonged. Then he covered her hand with his, deeply thrilled at this recollection of his past. She pulled her hand away, but why? Had she let him touch her for a minute, the warmth, the respite, would have lasted for weeks. "Well," she said, regaining her composure, her beauty, he thought.

The light in the room was unkind, but she was

equal to its harshness. She had been an authenticated beauty. Several photographers had asked her to model, although her breasts, marvelous for nursing and love, were a little too big for that line of work. "I'm much too shy, much too lazy," she had said. She had accepted the compliment; her beauty had been documented. "You know," his son had said, "I can't talk to Mummy when there's a mirror in the room. She's really balmy about her looks." Narcissus was a man and he couldn't make the switch, but she had, maybe twelve or fourteen times, stood in front of the full-length mirror in their bedroom and asked him, "Is there another woman of my age in this county who is as beautiful as I?" She had been naked, overwhelmingly so, and he had thought this an invitation, but when he touched her she said, "Stop fussing with my breasts. I'm beautiful." She was, too. He knew that after she'd left, whoever had seen her—the turnkey, for instance—would say, "If that was your wife you're lucky. Outside the movies I never seen anyone so beautiful."

If she was Narcissa did the rest of the Freudian doctrine follow? He had never, within his limited judgment, taken this very seriously. She had spent three weeks in Rome with her old roommate Maria Lippincott Hastings Guglielmi. Three marriages, a fat settlement for each, and a very unsavory sexual reputation. They then had no maid and he and Peter had cleaned the house, laid and lighted fires, and bought flowers to celebrate her return from Italy. He met her at Kennedy. The plane was late. It was after midnight. When he bent to kiss her she averted her face and pulled down the floppy brim of her new Roman hat. He got her bags, got the car and they started home. "You seem to have had a marvelous time," he said. "I have never," she said, "been so happy in my life." He jumped to no conclusions. The fires would be burning, the flowers gleaming. In that part of the world the ground was covered with dirty snow. "Was there any snow in Rome?" he asked. "Not in the city," she said. "There was a little snow on the Via Cassia. I didn't see it. I read about it in the paper. Nothing so revolting as this."

He carried the bags into the living room. Peter was there in his pajamas. She embraced him and cried a little. The fires and the flowers missed her by a mile. He could try to kiss her again, but he knew that he might get a right to the jaw. "Can I get you a drink?" he asked, making the offer in a voice that rose. "I guess so," she said, dropping an octave. "Campari," she said. "*Limone*?" he asked. "*Sì, sì*," she said, "un spritz." He got the ice, the lemon peel, and handed her the drink. "Put it on the table," she said. "Campari will remind me of my lost happiness." She went into the kitchen, wet a sponge and began to wash the door of the refrigerator. "We cleaned the place," he said with genuine sadness. "Peter and I cleaned the place. Peter mopped the kitchen floor." "Well, you seem to have forgotten the refrigerator door," she said. "If there are angels in heaven," he said, "and if they are women, I expect they must put down their harps quite frequently to mop drainboards, refrigerator doors, any enameled surface. It seems to be a secondary female characteristic." "Are you crazy?" she asked. "I don't know what you're talking about." His cock, so recently ready for fun, retreated from Waterloo to Paris and from Paris to Elba.

"Almost everyone I love has called me crazy," he said. "What I'd like to talk about is love." "Oh, is that it," she said. "Well, here you go." She put her thumbs into her ears, wagged her fingers, crossed her eyes and made a loud farting sound with her tongue. "I wish you wouldn't make faces," he said. "I wish you wouldn't look like that," she said. "Thank God you can't see the way you look." He said nothing more since he knew that Peter was listening.

It took her that time about ten days to come around. It was after a cocktail party and before a dinner. They took a nap, she in his arms. They were one, he thought. The fragrant skein of her hair lay across his face. Her breathing was heavy. When she woke she touched his face and asked: "Did I snore?" "Terribly," he said, "you sounded like a chain saw." "It was a lovely sleep," she said, "I love to sleep in your arms." Then they made love. His imagery for a big orgasm was winning the sailboat race, the Renaissance, high mountains. "Christ, that felt good," she said. "What time is it?" "Seven," he said. "When are we due?" "Eight." "You've had your bath, I'll take mine." He dried her with a Kleenex and passed her a lighted cigarette. He followed her into the bathroom and sat on the shut toilet seat while she washed her back with a brush. "I forgot to tell you," he said. "Liza sent us a wheel of Brie." "That's nice," she said, "but you know what? Brie gives me terribly loose bowels." He hitched up his genitals and crossed his legs. "That's funny," he said. "It constipates me." That was their marriage then—not the highest paving of the stair, the clatter of Italian fountains, the wind in the alien olive trees, but this: a jay-naked male and female discussing their bowels.

One more time. It was when they still bred dogs. Hannah, the bitch, had whelped a litter of eight. Seven were in the kennel behind the house. One, a sickly runt who would die, had been let in. Farragut was waked from a light sleep at around three, by the noise of the puppy vomiting or defecating. He slept naked and naked he left the bed, trying not to disturb Marcia, and went down to the living room. There was a mess under the piano. The puppy was trembling. "That's all right, Gordo," he said. Peter had named the puppy Gordon Cooper. It was that long ago. He got a mop, a bucket and some paper towels and crawled bare-ass under the piano to clean up the shit. He had disturbed her and he heard her come down the stairs. She wore a transparent nightgown and everything was to be seen. "I'm sorry I disturbed you," he said. "Gordo had an accident." "I'll help," she said. "You needn't," he said. "It's almost done." "But I want to," she said. On her hands and knees, she joined him under the piano. When it was done she stood and struck her head on that part of the piano that overlaps the bulk of the instrument. "Oh," she said. "Did you hurt yourself?" he asked. "Not terribly," she said. "I hope I won't have a bump or a shiner." "I'm sorry, my darling," he said. He stood, embraced her, kissed her and they made love on the sofa. He lighted a cigarette for her and they returned to bed. But it wasn't much after this that he stepped into the kitchen to get some ice and found her embracing and kissing Sally Midland, with whom she did crewelwork twice a week. He thought the embrace was not platonic and he detested Sally. "Excuse me," he said. "What for?" she asked. "I broke wind," he said. That was nasty and he knew it. He carried the ice tray into the pantry. She was silent during dinner and for the rest of the evening. When they woke the next day—Saturday—he asked: "Good morning, darling?" "Shit," she said. She put on her wrapper and went to the kitchen, where he heard her kick the refrigerator and then the dishwasher. "I hate you broken-down fucking second-rate appliances," she shouted. "I hate, hate, hate this fucking dirty old-fashioned kitchen. I dreamt that I dwelt in marble halls." This was ominous, he knew, and the omens meant that he would get no breakfast. When she was distempered she regarded the breakfast eggs as if she had laid and hatched them. The egg, the egg for breakfast! The egg was like some sibyl in an Attic drama. "May I have eggs for breakfast?" he had once asked, years and years ago. "Do you expect me to prepare breakfast in this House of Usher?" she had asked. "Could I cook myself some eggs?" he asked. "You may not," she said. "You will make such a mess in this ruin that it will take hours for me to clean it up." On such a morning, he knew, he would be lucky to get a cup of coffee. When he dressed and went down, her face was still very dark and this made him feel much more grievous than hungry. How could he repair this? He saw out the window that there had been a frost, the first. The sun had risen, but the white hoarfrost stood in the shadow of the house and the trees with a Euclidian preciseness. It was after the first frost that you cut the fox grapes she liked for jelly, not much bigger than raisins, black, gamy; he thought that perhaps a bag of fox grapes would do the trick. He was scrupulous about the sexual magic of tools. This could be anxiety or the fact that they had once summered in southwestern Ireland, where tools had been male and female. He would, carrying a basket and shears, have felt like a transvestite. He chose a burlap sack and a hunting knife. He went into the woods—half or three-quarters of a mile from the house—to where there was a stand of fox grapes against a stand of pines. The exposure was due east and they were ripe, blackish-purple and rimmed with frost in the shade. He cut them with his manly knife and slapped them into the crude sack. He cut them for her, but who was she? Sally Midland's lover? Yes, yes, yes! Face the facts. What he faced was either the biggest of falsehoods or the biggest of truths, but in any case a sense of reasonableness enveloped and supported him. But if she loved Sally Midland, didn't he love Chucky Drew? He liked to be with Chucky Drew, but when they stood side by side in the shower he thought that Chucky looked like a diseased chicken, with flabby arms like the arms of those women who used to play bridge with his mother. He had not loved a man, he thought, since he had left the Boy Scouts. So, with his bag of wild grapes, he returned to the house, burs on his trousers, his brow bitten by the last flies of that year. She had gone back to bed. She lay there with her face in the pillow. "I picked some grapes," he said. "We had the first frost last night. I picked some fox grapes for jelly." "Thank you," she said, into the pillow. "I'll leave them in the kitchen," he said. He spent the rest of the day preparing the house for winter. He took down the screens and put up the storm windows, banked the rhododendrons with raked and acid oak leaves, checked the oil level in the fuel tank and sharpened his skates. He worked along with numerous hornets who bumped against the eaves, looking, even as he, for some sanctuary for the coming ice age. . . .

"It was partly because we stopped doing things together," he said. "We used to do so much together. We used to sleep together, travel together, ski, skate, sail, go to concerts, we did everything together, we watched the World Series and drank beer together although neither of us likes beer, not in this country. That was the year Lomberg, whatever his name was, missed a no-hitter by half an inning. You cried. I did too. We cried together."

"You had your fix," she said. "We couldn't do that together."

"But I was clean for six months," he said. "It didn't make any difference. Cold turkey. It nearly killed me."

"Six months is not a lifetime," she said, "and anyhow, how long ago was that?"

"Your point," he said.

"How are you now?"

"I'm down from forty milligrams to ten. I get methadone at nine every morning. A pansy deals it out. He wears a hairpiece."

"Is he on the make?"

"I don't know. He asked me if I liked opera."

"You don't, of course."

"That's what I told him."

"That's good. I wouldn't want to be married to a

homosexual, having already married a homicidal drug addict."

"I did not kill my brother."

"You struck him with a fire iron. He died."

"I struck him with a fire iron. He was drunk. He hit his head on the hearth."

"All penologists say that all convicts claim innocence."

"Confucius say . . ."

"You're so superficial, Farragut. You've always been a lightweight."

"I did not kill my brother."

"Shall we change the subject?"

"Please."

"When do you think you'll be clean?"

"I don't know. I find it difficult to imagine cleanliness. I can claim to imagine this, but it would be false. It would be as though I had claimed to reinstall myself in some afternoon of my youth."

"That's why you're a lightweight."

"Yes."

He did not want a quarrel, not there, not ever again with her. He had observed, in the last year of their marriage, that the lines of a quarrel were as ritualistic as the words and the sacrament of holy matrimony. "I don't have to listen to your shit anymore," she had screamed. He was astonished, not at her hysteria, but at the fact that she had taken the words out of his mouth. "You've ruined my life, you've ruined my life," she screamed. "There is nothing on earth as cruel as a rotten marriage." This was all on the tip of his tongue. But then, listening for her to continue to anticipate his thinking, he heard her voice, deepened and softened with true grief, begin a variation that was not in his power. "You are the biggest mistake I ever made," she said softly. "I thought that my life was one hundred percent frustration, but when you killed your brother I saw that I had underestimated my problems."

When she spoke of frustration she sometimes meant the frustration of her career as a painter, which had begun and ended by her winning second prize at an art show in college twenty-five years ago. He had been called a bitch by a woman he deeply loved and he had always kept this possibility in mind. The woman had called him a bitch when they were both jay-naked on the upper floor of a good hotel. She then kissed him and said: "Let's pour whiskey all over one another and drink it." They had, and he could not doubt the judgment of such a woman. So bitchily, perhaps, he went over her career as a painter. When they first met she had lived in a studio and occupied herself mostly with painting. When they married, the *Times* had described her as a painter and every apartment and house they lived in had a studio. She painted and painted and painted. When guests came for dinner they were shown her paintings. She had her paintings photographed and sent to galleries. She had exhibited in public parks, streets and flea markets. She had carried her paintings up Fifty-seventh Street, Sixty-third Street, Seventy-second Street, she had applied for grants, awards, admission to subsidized painting colonies, she had painted and painted and painted, but her work had never been received with any enthusiasm at all. He understood, he tried to understand, bitch that he was.

This was her vocation, as powerful, he guessed, as the love of God, and as with some star-crossed priest, her prayers misfired. This had its rueful charms.

Her passion for independence had reached into her manipulation of their joint checking account. The independence of women was nothing at all new to him. His experience was broad, if not exceptional. His great-grandmother had been twice around the Horn, under sail. She was supercargo, of course, the captain's wife, but this had not protected her from great storms at sea, loneliness, the chance of mutiny and death or worse. His grandmother had wanted to be a fireman. She was pre-Freudian, but not humorless about this. "I love bells," she said, "ladders, hoses, the thunder and crash of water. Why can't I volunteer for the fire department?" His mother had been an unsuccessful business-woman, the manager of tearooms, restaurants, dress shops and at one time the owner of a factory that turned out handbags, painted cigarette boxes and door-stops. Marcia's thrust for independence was not, he knew, the burden of his company but the burden of history.

He had caught on to the checkbook manipulation almost as soon as it began. She had a little money of her own, but scarcely enough to pay for her clothes. She was dependent upon him and was determined, since she couldn't correct this situation, to conceal it. She had begun to have tradesmen cash checks and then claim that the money had been spent for the maintenance of the house. Plumbers, electricians, carpenters and painters didn't quite understand what she was doing, but she was solvent and they didn't mind cashing her checks. When Farragut discovered this he knew that her motive was independence. She must have known that he knew. Since they were both knowledgeable, what was the point of bringing it up unless he wanted a shower of tears—which was the last thing he wanted.

"And how," he asked, "is the house? How is Indian Hill?" He did not use the possessive pronoun—My house, Your house, Our house. It was still his house and would be until she got a divorce. She didn't reply. She did not draw on her gloves finger by finger, or touch her hair, or resort to any of the soap opera chestnuts used to express contempt. She was sharper than that. "Well," she said, "it's nice to have a dry toilet seat."

He jogged out of the visitors' room and up the stairs to cellblock F. He hung his white shirt on a hanger and went to the window, where, for the space of about a foot, he could focus on two steps of the entrance and the sidewalk the visitors would take on their way to cars, taxis or the train. He waited for them to emerge like a waiter in an American-plan hotel waiting for the dining room doors to open, like a lover, like a drought-ruined farmer waiting for rain, but without the sense of the universality of waiting.

They appeared—one, three, four, two—twenty-seven in all. It was a weekday. Chicanos, blacks, whites, his upper-class wife with her bell-shaped coif— whatever was fashionable that year. She had been to the hairdresser before she came to prison. Had she said as much? "I'm not going to a party, I'm going to jail to see my husband." He remembered the women in the sea before Ann Ecbatan's coming out. They all swam a breast stroke to keep their hair dry. Now some of the visitors carried paper bags in which they brought home the contraband they had tried to pass on to their loved ones. They were free, free to run, jump, fuck, drink, book a seat on the Tokyo plane. They were free and yet they moved so casually through this precious element that it seemed wasted on them. There was no appreciation of freedom in the way they moved. A man stooped to pull up his socks. A woman rooted through her handbag to make sure she had the keys. A younger woman, glancing at the overcast sky, put up a green umbrella. An old and very ugly woman dried her tears with a scrap of paper. These were their constraints, the signs of their confinement, but there was some naturalness, some unself-consciousness about their imprisonment that he, watching them between bars, cruelly lacked.

This was not pain, nothing so simple and clear as that. All he could identify was some disturbance in his tear ducts, a blind, unthinking wish to cry. Tears were easy; a good ten-minute hand job. He wanted to cry and howl. He was among the living dead. There were no words, no living words, to suit this grief, this cleavage. He was primordial man confronted with romantic love. His eyes began to water as the last of the visitors, the last shoe, disappeared. He sat on his bunk and took in his right hand the most interesting, worldly, responsive and nostalgic object in the cell. "Speed it up," said Chicken Number Two. "You only got eight minutes to chow."

Cellblock F was only half tenanted. Most of the toilets and locks on the upper tier were broken and these were empty. Nothing but the cell locks really worked and the toilet in Farragut's cell flushed itself noisily and independently. The air of obsolescence—the feeling that these must surely be the last days of incarceration—was strong. Of the twenty men in F, Farragut, at the end of two weeks, fell into a family group that consisted of Chicken Number Two, Bumpo, the Stone, the Cuckold, Ransome and Tennis. This organization was deeply mysterious. Ransome was a very tall and a handsome man who was supposed to have murdered his father. Farragut had quickly learned never to ask a comrade what he was doing in Falconer. It would be a stupid violation of the terms on which they lived with one another, and in any case the truth was not in them. Ransome was laconic. He spoke to almost no one but the Stone, who was helpless. Everyone talked about the Stone. Some criminal organization had pierced his eardrums with an ice pick. They had then framed him, bought him a long sentence and given him a two-hundred-dollar hearing machine. This was a canvas carrier that hung from his shoulders by straps. It contained a plastic flesh-colored receiver, a pipe to his right ear and four batteries. Ransome guided the Stone to and from mess, urged him to wear his hearing appliance and changed his batteries when they faded. He almost never spoke to anyone else.

Tennis had come on hard on Farragut's second day, early in the morning when they had swept their cells and were waiting for chow. "I'm Lloyd Haversham, Jr.," he said. "Does that name ring a bell? No? They call me Tennis. I thought you might know because you look like the sort of man who might play tennis. I won the

Spartanburg doubles, twice in a row. I'm the second man in the history of tennis to have done this. I learned on private courts, of course. I've never played on a public court. I'm listed in the sports encyclopedia, the dictionary of sports greats, I'm a member of the tennis academy and I was cover story in the March issue of *Racquets*. *Racquets* is the leading publication of the tennis equipment industry." While he talked, Tennis displayed all the physical business of a hard sell— hands, shoulders, pelvis, everything was in motion. "I'm in here because of a clerical error, an error in banking. I'm a visitor, a transient, I see the parole board in a few days and I'll be out then. I deposited thirteen thousand dollars in the Bank for Mutual Savings on the morning of the ninth and wrote three checks for two hundred dollars before the deposit had cleared. By accident I used my roommate's checkbook —he was runner-up in the Spartanburg doubles and never forgave me for my victory. All a man needs is a little jealousy and a clerical error—bad luck—and they throw him into jail, but I'll leap the net in a week or two. This is more of a goodbye than a hello but hello anyhow!" Tennis, like most of them, talked in his sleep and Farragut had heard him asking: "Have you been taken care of? Have you been taken care of?" Bumpo explained this to Farragut. Tennis's athletic career was thirty years in the past and he had been picked up for check forgery when he was working as a delicatessen clerk. Bumpo had this to say about Tennis, but he said nothing about himself, although he was the cellblock celebrity and was supposed to have been the second man to hijack an airplane. He had forced a pilot to fly from Minneapolis to Cuba and was in on an eighteen-year sentence for kidnapping. Bumpo never mentioned this or anything else about himself excepting a large ring he wore, set with a diamond or a piece of glass. "It's worth twenty thousand," he said. The price varied from day to day. "I'd sell it, I'd sell it tomorrow if somebody'd guarantee me it would save a life. I mean if there was some very old and lonely and hungry person whose life I could save, well, then I'd sell it. Of course, I'd have to see the documents. Or if there was some little girl who was defenseless and all alone and I was sure that nobody or nothing else in the world could save her life, well, then I'd give her my stone. But first I'd want to see the documents. I'd want to have affidavits and photographs and birth certificates, but if it could be proven to me that my rock was the only thing that was between her and the grave, well, then she could have it in ten minutes."

Chicken Number Two talked about his brilliant career as a jewel thief in New York, Chicago and Los Angeles, and while he talked in his sleep more than the rest of them, there was in his talk a refrain. "Don't ask her for a lower price," he would shout. His voice was vehement and irritable. "I told you, don't ask her for a lower price. She ain't going to give it to you for a lower price, so don't ask." When he talked about his career he did not detail his successes. He spoke mostly about his charm. "The reason I was so great was my charm. I was very charming. Everybody knew I had class. And willingness, I had willingness. I give the impression of a very willing person. Anybody asks me to get anything, I give them the impression that I'll try. Get me the Niagara Falls, they say. Get me the Empire State Building. Yes sir, I always say, yes sir, I'll try. I got class."

The Cuckold, like Tennis, came on hard. Farragut had not been a member of the family for a week before the Cuckold paid him a call. He was a fat man with a very pink face, thin hair and a galling and exaggerated smile. The most interesting thing about him was that he ran a business. He paid a package of mentholated cigarettes for every two spoons that anyone could lift from the mess hall. In the shop he turned the spoons into bracelets, and Walton, the cell corporal, kited these out in his underwear and fenced them at a gift shop in the nearest city, where they were advertised as having been created by a man who was condemned to death. They sold for twenty-five dollars. With these profits he kept his cell full of canned hams, chickens, sardines, peanut butter, crackers and pasta, which he used as bait to get his comrades to listen to his stories about his wife. "Let me entertain you with a nice slice of ham," he said to Farragut. "Sit down, sit down, and have a nice slice of ham, but first let me tell you what I'm in here for. I iced my wife by mistake. The night I iced her was the night she told me none of the three kids was mine. Also she told me that the two abortions I paid for and the miscarriage wasn't mine either. That's when I iced her. Even when things were going good she couldn't be trusted. Like there was this week or two when we were just fucking all the time. I was in sales but it was an off-season and we just stayed in the house fucking and eating and drinking. So then she said what we needed was a vacation from fucking one another and I could see what she meant. I was really in love. She said wouldn't it be great if we was away for a couple of weeks and how wonderful it would be when we was reunited. Wouldn't it. So I saw what she meant and I went back on the road for a couple of weeks but one night in South Dakota I got drunk and laid a stranger and I felt very guilty so when I come home and took off my pants I felt I had to confess to her that I had been impure and so I did. So then she kissed me and said it didn't matter and she was glad I had confessed because she had a confession to make herself. She said that on the day I left she got a cab to go to the other side of town to see her sister and this cabdriver had such sparkly black eyes that they seemed to stick into her and so she scored with the cabdriver when he got off duty at ten. And the next day she went to Melcher's to buy some cat food and there was a traffic pileup to which she was a witness and when this handsome state trooper was questioning her he asked if he could continue the questioning at home and so she scored with him. So then that night, that very night, an old high school chum showed up and she scored, wet-decks, with him. Then the next morning, the very next morning, when she was getting gas at Harry's she got the hots for this new gas pumper and he comes over to the house on his lunch hour. So at about that time I got back into my pants and went out of the house and down to the bar on the corner and stayed there for about two hours but at the end of two hours I was back in bed with her." "You were going to give me a piece of ham," said Farragut. "Oh, yes," said the Cuckold. He was both stingy and greedy, and Farragut got only a thin, small slice of ham. Chicken bargained with the Cuckold and wouldn't go into his cell until he had been promised a set quantity of food.

Farragut queued up for supper between Bumpo and Tennis that night. They had rice, franks, bread, oleomargarine and half a canned peach. He palmed three slices of bread for his cat and jogged up to cellblock F. Jogging gave him the illusion of freedom. Tiny was sitting down to his supper of outside food at his desk at the end of the block. He had on his plate a nice London broil, three baked potatoes, a can of peas and on another plate a whole store cake. Farragut sighed loudly when he smelled the meat. Food was a recently revealed truth in his life. He had reasoned that the Holy Eucharist was nutritious if you got enough of it. In some churches, at some times, they had baked the bread—hot, fragrant and crusty—in the chancel. Eat this in memory of me. Food had something to do with his beginnings as a Christian and a man. To cut short a breast-feeding, he had read somewhere, was traumatic and from what he remembered of his mother she might have yanked her breast out of his mouth in order not to be late for her bridge game; but this was coming close to self-pity and he had tried to leach self-pity out of his emotional spectrum. Food was food, hunger was hunger and his half-empty belly and the perfume of roast meat established a rapport that it would take the devil to cut in two. "Eat good," he said to Tiny. A telephone was ringing in another room. The TV was on and the majority had picked, through a rigged ballot, some game show. The irony of TV, played out against any form of life or death, was superficial and fortuitous.

So as you lay dying, as you stood at the barred window watching the empty square, you heard the voice of a man, a half-man, the sort of person you wouldn't have spoken to at school or college, the victim of a bad barber, tailor and makeup artist, exclaim: "We present with pleasure to Mrs. Charles Alcorn, of 11,235 275th Boulevard, the four-door cathedral-size refrigerator containing two hundred pounds of prime beef and enough staples to feed a family of six for two months. This includes pet food. Don't you cry, Mrs. Alcorn—oh, darling, don't you cry, don't you cry. . . . And to the other contestants a complete kit of the sponsor's product." The time for banal irony, the voice-over, he thought, is long gone. Give me the chords, the deep rivers, the unchanging profundity of nostalgia, love and death. Tiny had begun to roar. He was usually a reasonable man, but now his voice was high, shattering, crazy. "You rat-fucking, cock-sucking, ass-tonguing, sneaky, stinking fleabag."

Obscenities recalled for Farragut the long-ago war with Germany and Japan. "In a fucking line-rifle company," he or anyone else might have said, "you get the fucking, malfunctioning M-1's, fucking '03's to simulate fucking carbines, fucking obsolete BAR's and fucking sixty-millimeter mortars where you have to set the fucking sight to bracket the fucking target." Obscenity worked on their speech like a tonic, giving it force and structure, but the word "fucking," so much later, had for Farragut the dim force of a recollection. "Fucking" meant M-1's, sixty-pound packs, landing nets, the stinking Pacific islands with Tokyo Rose coming over the radio. Now Tiny's genuine outburst unearthed a past, not very vivid because there was no sweetness in it, but a solid, memorable four years of his life. The Cuckold passed and Farragut asked, "What's wrong with Tiny?" "Oh, don't you know," said the Cuckold. "He had just begun his dinner when the deputy called him on the outside phone to check on work sheets. When he got back, a couple of cats, big cats, had finished off his steak and potatoes, shit in his plate and were halfway through his cake. He tore the head off one of them. The other got away. When he was tearing off the cat's head he got very badly bitten. He's bleeding and bleeding. I guess he's gone to the infirmary."

If prisons were constructed to make any living thing happy it might have been cats, although the sententiousness of this observation made Farragut irritable. But the fact was that trained men with drawing boards, hod carriers, mortar and stone had constructed buildings to deny their own kind a fair measure of freedom. The cats profited most. Even the fattest of them, the sixty-pounders, could ease their way between the bars, where there were plenty of rats and mice for the hunters, lovelorn men for the tender and the teases, and franks, meatballs, day-old bread and oleomargarine to eat.

Farragut had seen the cats of Luxor, Cairo and Rome, but with everybody going around the world these days and writing cards and sometimes books about it, there wasn't much point in linking the shadowy cats of prison to the shadowy cats of the ancient world. As a dog breeder he had not much liked cats, but he had changed. There were more cats in Falconer than there were convicts, and there were two thousand convicts. Make it four thousand cats. Their smell overwhelmed everything, but they checked the rat and mouse population. Farragut had a favorite. So did everybody else—some had as many as six. Some of the men's wives brought them Kitty Chow—stuff like that. Loneliness taught the intransigent to love their cats as loneliness can change anything on earth. They were warm, they were hairy, they were living, and they gave fleeting glimpses of demonstrativeness, intelligence, uniqueness and sometimes grace and beauty. Farragut called his cat Bandit because—black and white—it had a mask like a stagecoach robber or a raccoon. "Hi, pussy," he said. He put the three pieces of bread on the floor. Bandit first licked the margarine off the bread and then, with feline niceness, ate the crusts, took a drink of water out of the toilet, finished the soft part and climbed onto Farragut's lap. His claws cut through the fatigues like the thorns of a rose. "Good Bandit, good Bandit. You know what, Bandit? My wife, my only wife, came to see me today and I don't know what in hell to think about the visit. I remember mostly watching her walk away from the place. Shit, Bandit, I love her." He worked behind the cat's ears with his thumb and third finger. Bandit purred loudly and shut his eyes. He had never figured out the cat's sex. He was reminded of the Chicanos in the visiting room. "It's a good thing you don't turn me on, Bandit. I used to have an awful time with my member. Once I climbed this mountain in the Abruzzi. Six thousand feet. The woods were supposed to be full of bears. That's why I climbed the mountain. To see the bears. There was a refuge on the top of the mountain and I got there just before dark. I went in and built a fire and ate the sandwiches I'd brought and drank some wine and got into my sleeping bag and looked around for sleep, but my Goddamned member was not in the mood for sleep at all. It was throbbing and asking where the action was, why we'd climbed this mountain with no rewards, what was my purpose and so forth. Then someone, some animal, started scratching at the door. It must have been a wolf or a bear. Except for me there wasn't anything else on the mountain. So then I said to my member, If that's a female wolf or a female bear, perhaps I can fix you up. This made it thoughtful for once, pensive, and I got to sleep but—"

Then the general alarm rang. Farragut had never heard it before and didn't know what it was called, but it was a racket, obviously meant to announce fires, riots, the climax and the end of things. It rang on and on, long after its usefulness as an announcement, a warning, an alert, an alarm, had come to an end. It sounded like some approach to craziness, it was out of control, it was in control, in possession, and then someone pulled a switch and there was that brief, brief sweetness that comes with the cessation of pain. Most of the cats had hidden and the wiser ones had taken off. Bandit was behind the toilet. Then the metal door rolled open and a bunch of guards came in, led by Tiny. They wore the yellow waterproofs they wore for fire drill and they all carried clubs.

"Any of you got cats in your cells throw them out,"

said Tiny. Two cats at the end of the block, thinking perhaps that Tiny had food, came toward him. One was big, one was little. Tiny raised his club, way in the air, and caught a cat on the completion of the falling arc, tearing it in two. At the same time another guard bashed in the head of the big cat. Blood, brains and offal splattered their yellow waterproofs and the sight of carnage reverberated through Farragut's dental work; caps, inlays, restorations, they all began to ache. He snapped his head around to see that Bandit had started for the closed door. He was pleased at this show of intelligence and by the fact that Bandit had spared him the confrontation that was going on between Tiny and Chicken Number Two: "Throw that cat out," said Tiny to Chicken. "You ain't going to kill my pussy," said Chicken. "You want six days cell lock," said Tiny. "You ain't going to kill my pussy," said Chicken. "Eight days cell lock," said Tiny. Chicken said nothing. He was hanging on to the cat. "You want the hole," said Tiny. "You want a month in the hole." "I'll come back and get it later," said one of the other men.

It was half and half. Half the cats cased the slaughter and made for the closed door. Half of them wandered around at a loss, sniffing the blood of their kind and sometimes drinking it. Two of the guards vomited and half a dozen cats got killed eating the vomit. The cats that hung around the door, waiting to be let out, were an easy target. When a third guard got sick Tiny said, "O.K., O.K., that's enough for tonight, but it don't give me back my London broil. Get the fire detail to clean this up." He signaled for the door to open and when it rolled back six or maybe ten cats escaped, giving to Farragut some reminder of the invincible.

The fire detail came in with waste cans, shovels and two lengths of hose. They sluiced down the block and shoveled up the dead cats. They sluiced down the cells as well and Farragut climbed onto his bunk, knelt there and said: "Blessed are the meek," but he couldn't remember what came next.

Farragut was a drug addict and felt that the consciousness of the opium eater was much broader, more vast and representative of the human condition than the consciousness of someone who had never experienced addiction. The drug he needed was a distillate of earth, air, water and fire. He was mortal and his addiction was a beautiful illustration of the bounds of his mortality. He had been introduced to drugs during a war on some island where the weather was suffocating, the jungle rot of his hairy parts was suppurating and the enemy were murderers. The company medic had ordered gallons of a sticky yellow cough syrup and every morning the "in" group drank a glass of this and went into combat, drugged and at peace with suffocation, suppuration and murder. This was followed by Benzedrine, and Benzedrine and his beer ration got him through the war and back to his own shores, his own home and his wife. He went guiltlessly from Benzedrine to heroin, encouraged in his addiction by almost every voice he heard. Yesterday was the age of anxiety, the age of the fish, and today, his day, his morning, was the mysterious and adventurous age of the needle. His generation was the generation of addiction. It was his school, his college, the flag under which he marched into battle. The declaration of addiction was in every paper, magazine and airborne voice. Addiction was the law of the prophets. When he began to teach, he and his department head would shoot up before the big lecture, admitting that what was expected of them from the world could be produced only by the essence of a flower. It was challenge and response. The new buildings of the university outstripped the human scale, the human imagination, the wildest human dreams. The bridges that he drove across to get to the university were the distillate of engineering computers, a sort of mechanical Holy Ghost. The planes that took him from his university to some other university arced luxuriously into an altitude where men would perish. There was no philosophical suture that could make anything but destructiveness of the sciences that were taught in the high buildings he could see from the windows of English and Philosophy. There were some men of such stupidity that they did not respond to these murderous contradictions and led lives that were without awareness and distinction. His memory of a life without drugs was like a memory of himself as a blond, half-naked youth in good flannels, walking on a white beach between the dark sea and a rank of leonine granite, and to seek out such a memory was contemptible. A life without drugs seemed in fact and in spirit a remote and despicable point in his past—binoculars upon telescopes, lens grating lens, employed to pick out a figure of no consequence on a long gone summer's day.

But in the vastness of his opium eater's consciousness was—no more than a grain of sand—the knowledge that if his inspired knowledge of the earth's drugs was severed, he would face a cruel and unnatural death. Congressmen and senators sometimes visited prison. They were seldom shown the methadone line, but twice when they had stumbled on this formation they had objected to the sweat of the taxpayers' brow being wasted to sustain convicted felons in their diseased addiction. Their protests had not been effective, but Farragut's feeling about visiting senators in prison had turned into a murderous hatred since these men might kill him. The fear of death is for all of us everywhere, but for the great intelligence of the opium eater it is beautifully narrowed into the crux of drugs. To starve to death, to burn or drown in the bliss of a great high, would be nothing at all. Drugs belonged to all exalted experience, thought Farragut. Drugs belonged in church. Take this in memory of me and be grateful, said the priest, laying an amphetamine on the kneeling man's tongue. Only the opium eater truly understands the pain of death. When one morning the orderly who gave Farragut his methadone sneezed, this was for Farragut an ominous and a dreadful sound. The orderly might come down with a cold, and considering the nature of the prison bureaucracy, there might not be anyone else who had permission to issue the drug. The sound of a sneeze meant death.

A search for contraband was called on Thursday and the cellblocks were off limits until after night chow. At around eight the names of the malefactors were announced. The Cuckold and Farragut were called and they went down to the deputy warden's office. Two spoons had been found, hidden in Farragut's toilet bowl. He was given six days cell lock. Farragut faced the sentence calmly by first considering the pain of confinement. He assured himself that he could stand confinement with composure. He was at that time the prison's chief typist, respected for his intelligence, efficiency and speed, and he had to face the possibility that in his absence some new typist might be put in his place in the shop and his slot, his job, his self-importance, would be eclipsed. Someone might have come in that afternoon on the bus who could fire off dittos at twice his speed and usurp his office, his chair, his desk and his lamp. Worried about the thrall of confinement and the threat of his self-esteem, Farragut went back to Tiny, gave him his penance slip and asked: "How will I get my fix?"

"I'll check," said Tiny. "They'll bring it up from the infirmary, I guess. You don't get nothing until tomorrow morning." Farragut didn't need methadone then, but the morning threatened to usurp the facts of the night. He undressed, got into bed and watched the news on TV. The news for the last two weeks had been dominated by a murderess. She had been given the usual characteristics. She and her husband lived in an expensive house in an exclusive community. The house was painted white, the grounds were planted with costly firs and the lawn and the hedges were beautifully maintained. Her character had been admired. She taught Sunday school and had been a den mother for the Girl Scouts. Her coffeecakes for the Trinity Church bake sale were famous and at PTA meetings she expressed herself with intelligence, character and charm. "Oh, she was so kind," her neighbors said, "so clean, so friendly, she loved him so that I can't imagine . . ." What they couldn't imagine was that she had murdered her husband, carefully drained his blood and flushed it down the toilet, washed him clean and begun to rectify and improve his physique. First she decapitated the corpse and replaced his head with the drained head of a second victim. She then replaced his genitals with the genitals of her third victim and his feet with the feet of her fourth. It was when she invited a neighbor in to see this perfect man that suspicions had been aroused. She then vanished. Offers to exploit the remains for commercial purposes were being considered, but nothing had been agreed upon. Night after night the fragments of the tale ended with a draw-away shot of the serene white house, the specimen planting and the velvet lawn.

Lying in bed, Farragut felt his anxiety beginning to mount. He would be denied his fix in the morning. He would die. He would be murdered. He then remembered the times when his life had been threatened.

Firstly his father, having written Farragut's name with his cock, had tried to erase the writing. One of his mother's favorite stories was of the night that Farragut's father brought a doctor to the house for dinner. Halfway through the dinner it turned out that the doctor was an abortionist and had been asked to dinner in order to kill Farragut. This, of course, he could not remember, but he could remember walking on a beach with his brother. This was on one of the Atlantic islands. At the tip of the island there was a narrows called Chilton Gut. "Swim?" his brother asked. His brother didn't like to swim, but Farragut, it was well known, would strip and jump into any body of water. He got out of his clothes and was wading into the sea when some stranger, a fisherman, came running up the beach, shouting: "Stop, stop! What do you think you're doing?" "I was going in for a dip," said Farragut. "You're crazy," the stranger said. "The tide is turning and even if the rip doesn't get you the sharks will. You can't ever swim here. They ought to put up a sign—but at the rip tide you wouldn't last a minute. You can't ever swim here. They waste all the taxpayers' money putting up traffic signs, speeding signs, yield signs, stop signs, but on a well-known deathtrap like this they don't have any sign at all." Farragut thanked the stranger and got back into his clothes. His brother had started down the beach. Eben must have jogged or run because he had put quite a distance between them. Farragut caught up with him and the first thing he asked was, "When is Louisa coming back from Denver? I know you've told me, but I've forgotten." "Tuesday," Eben said. "She's staying over for Ruth's wedding." So they walked back to the house, talking about Louisa's visit. Farragut remembered being happy at the fact that he was alive. The sky was blue.

At a rehabilitation center in Colorado where Farragut had been confined to check his addiction, the doctors discovered that heroin had damaged his heart. His cure lasted thirty-eight days and before he was discharged he was given his instructions. He was being discharged as an outpatient. Because of his heart he could not, for six weeks, climb stairs, drive a car or exert himself in any way. He must avoid strenuous changes in temperature and above all excitement. Excitement of any sort would kill him. The doctor then used the classic illustration of the man who shoveled snow, entered a hot house and quarreled with his wife. It was as quick as a bullet through the head. Farragut flew east and his flight was uneventful. He got a cab to their apartment, where Marcia let him in. "Hi," he said and bent to kiss her, but she averted her face. "I'm an outpatient," he said. "A salt-free diet—not really salt-free, but no salt added. I can't climb stairs or drive a car and I do have to avoid excitement. It seems easy enough. Maybe we could go to the beach."

Marcia walked down the long hall to their bedroom and slammed the door. The noise of the sound was explosive and in case he had missed this she opened the door and slammed it again. The effect on his heart was immediate. He became faint, dizzy and short-winded. He staggered to the sofa in the living room and lay down. He was in too much pain and fear to realize that the homecoming of a drug addict was not romantic. He fell asleep. The daylight had begun to go when he regained consciousness. His heart was still drumming, his vision was cloudy and he was very weak and frightened. He heard Marcia open the door to their room and come down the hall. "Is there anything I can get you?" she asked. Her tone was murderous.

"Some sort of kindness," he said. He was helpless. "A little kindness."

"Kindness?" she asked. "Do you expect kindness from me at a time like this? What have you ever done to deserve kindness? What have you ever given me? Drudgery. A superficial and a meaningless life. Dust. Cobwebs. Cars and cigarette lighters that don't work. Bathtub rings, unflushed toilets, an international renown for sexual depravity, clinical alcoholism and drug addiction, broken arms, legs, brain concussions and now a massive attack of heart failure. That's what you've given me to live with, and now you expect kindness." The drumming of his heart worsened, his vision got dimmer and he fell asleep, but when he awoke Marcia was cooking something in the kitchen and he was still alive.

Eben entered again. It was at a party in a New York brownstone. Some guests were leaving and he stood in an open window, shouting goodbye. It was a large window and he was standing on the sill. Below him was an areaway with an iron fence of palings, cast to look like spears. As he stood in the window, someone gave him a swift push. He jumped or fell out the window, missed the iron spears and landed on his knees on the paving. One of the departing guests returned and helped him to his feet and he went on talking about when they would meet again. He did this to avoid looking back at the window to see, if he might, who had pushed him. That he didn't want to know. He had sprained an ankle and bruised a knee, but he refrained from thinking about the incident again. Many years later, walking in the woods, Eben had suddenly asked: "Do you remember that party at Sarah's when you got terribly drunk and someone pushed you out the window?" "Yes," said Farragut. "I've never told you who it was," said Eben. "It was that man from Chicago." Farragut thought that his brother had incriminated himself with this remark, but Eben seemed to feel exonerated. He braced his shoulders, lifted his head to the light and began to kick the leaves on the path vigorously.

The lights and the TV went off. Tennis began to ask: "Have you been taken care of? Have you been taken care of?" Farragut, lying on his cot thinking of the morning and his possible death, thought that the dead, compared to the imprisoned, would have some advantages. The dead would at least have panoramic memories and regrets, while he, as a prisoner, found his memories of the shining world to be broken, intermittent and dependent upon chance smells—grass, shoe leather, the odor of piped water in the showers. He possessed some memories, but they were eclipsed and indisposed. Waking in the morning, he cast wildly and desperately around for a word, a metaphor, a touch or smell that would grant him a bearing, but he was left mostly with methadone and his unruly keel. He seemed, in prison, to be a traveler and he had traveled in enough strange countries to recognize this keen alienation. It was the sense that on waking before dawn, everything, beginning with the dream from which he waked, was alien. He had dreamed in another language and felt on waking the texture and smell of strange bedclothes. From the window came the strange smell of strange fuels. He bathed in strange and rusty water, wiped his ass on strange and barbarous toilet paper and climbed down unfamiliar stairs to be served a strange and profoundly offensive breakfast. That was travel. It was the same here. Everything he saw, touched, smelled and dreamed of was cruelly alien, but this continent or nation in which he might spend the rest of his living days had no flag, no anthem, no monarch, president, taxes, boundaries or graves.

He slept poorly and felt haggard when he woke. Chicken Number Two brought him gruel and coffee, but his heart was moving along with his watch. If the methadone didn't come at nine he would begin to die. It would not be anything that he could walk into, like an electric chair or a noose. At five minutes to nine he began to shout at Tiny. "I want my fix, it's time for my fix, just let me get down to the infirmary and get my fix." "Well, he has to take care of the line down there," Tiny said. "Home deliveries don't come until later." "Maybe they don't make home deliveries," said Farragut. He sat on his cot, closed his eyes and tried to force himself into unconsciousness. This lasted a few minutes. Then he roared: "Get me my fix, for Jesus Christ's sake!" Tiny went on figuring work sheets, but Farragut could barely see him. The rest of the men who hadn't gone to shop began to watch. There was no one else in cell lock but the Cuckold. Then Chisholm, the deputy warden, came in with two other assholes. "I hear you got a withdrawal show scheduled," he said. "Yeah," said Tiny. "It's not my idea." He didn't look up from his work sheets. "Take any empty table. The floor show's about to begin."

Farragut had begun to sweat from his armpits, crotch and brow. Then the sweat flowed down his ribs and soaked his trousers. His eyes were burning. He could still marshal the percentiles. He would lose fifty percent vision. When the sweat was in full flood, he began to shake. This began with his hands. He sat on them, but then his head began to wag. He stood. He was shaking all over. Then his right arm flew out. He pulled it back. His left knee jerked up into the air. He pushed it down, but it went up again and began to go up and down like a piston. He fell and beat his head on the floor, trying to achieve the reasonableness of pain. Pain would give him peace. When he realized that he could not reach pain this way, he began the enormous struggle to hang himself. He tried fifteen or a million times before he was able to get his hand on his belt buckle. His hand flew away and after another long struggle he got it back to the buckle and unfastened it. Then, on his knees, with his head still on the floor, he jerked the belt out of the loops. The sweat had stopped. Convulsions of cold racked him. No longer even on his knees, but moving over the floor like a swimmer, he got to the chair, looped the buckle onto itself for a noose and fastened the belt to a nail on the chair. He was trying to strangle himself when Chisholm said: "Cut the poor prick down and get his fix." Tiny unlocked the cell door. Farragut couldn't see much, but he could see this, and the instant the cell was unlocked he sprang to his feet, collided with Tiny and was halfway out the cell and running for the infirmary when Chisholm brained him with a chair. He came to in the infirmary with his left leg in a plaster cast and half his head in bandages. Tiny was there in civilian clothes. "Farragut, Farragut," he asked, "why is you an addict?"

Farragut didn't reply. Tiny patted him on the head. "I'll bring you in some fresh tomatoes tomorrow. My wife puts up fifty jars of tomato sauce. We have tomatoes for breakfast, lunch and supper. But I still got tomatoes left over. I'll bring some in tomorrow. You want anything else?"

"No, thank you," said Farragut. "I'd like some tomatoes."

"Why is you an addict?" asked Tiny, and he went away.

Farragut was not disconcerted by the question, but he was provoked. It was only natural that he should be an addict. He had been raised by people who dealt in contraband. Not hard drugs, but unlicensed spiritual, intellectual and erotic stimulants. He was the citizen, the product of some border principality such as Liechtenstein. His background lacked the mountainous scenery, but his passport was fat with visas, he dealt in spiritual contraband, spoke four languages poorly and knew the words to four national anthems. Once when he was sitting in a café in Kitzbühel with his brother, listening to a band concert, Eben suddenly sprang to his feet and clapped his Tyrolean hat over his heart. "What's up?" Farragut asked, and Eben said, "They are about to play the national anthem." What the band was about to play was "Home on the Range," but Farragut remembered this to illustrate the fact that his family had endeavored to be versatile at every political, spiritual and erotic level. It helped to explain the fact that he was an addict.

Farragut could remember his mother coming down a circular staircase in a coral-colored dress heavily embroidered with pearls on her way to hear *Tosca;* and he could remember her pumping gas on the main road to Cape Cod at that memorable point in the landscape where scrub pine takes over and the nearness of the Great Atlantic Ocean can be read in the pallor of the sky and the salt air. His mother didn't actually wear tennis sneakers, but she wore some kind of health shoe and her dress was much lower in the bow than in the stern. He could remember her casually and repeatedly regretting invitations to dine with the Trenchers, who were famous in the village for having, in the space of a week, bought both a pipe organ and a yacht. The Trenchers were millionaires—they were arrivistes—they had a butler; but then, the Farraguts had run through several butlers—Mario, Fender and Chadwick —and now claimed to enjoy setting their own table. The Farraguts were the sort of people who had lived in a Victorian mansion and when this was lost had moved back to the family homestead. This included a shabby and splendid eighteenth-century house and the franchise on two Socony gas pumps that stood in front of the house where Grandmother's famous rose garden had been. When the news got out that they had lost all their money and were going to run a gas station, Farragut's Aunt Louisa came directly to the house and, standing in the hallway, exclaimed: "You cannot pump gasoline!" "Why not?" asked Farragut's mother. Aunt Louisa's chauffeur came in and put a box of tomatoes on the floor. He wore puttees. "Because," said Aunt Louisa, "you will lose all your friends." "To the contrary," said Farragut's mother. "I shall discover precisely who they are."

The cream of the post-Freudian generation were addicts. The rest were those psychiatric reconstructions you used to see in the back of unpopular rooms at cocktail parties. They seemed to be intact, but if you touched them in the wrong place at the wrong time they would collapse all over the floor like a spatchcocked card trick. Drug addiction is symptomatic. Opium eaters *know*. Farragut remembered a fellow opium eater named Polly, whose mother was an on-again off-again recording and club singer. Her name was Corinne. When Corinne was way down and struggling to get back, Farragut took Polly to her mother's big breakthrough in Las Vegas. The breakthrough was successful and Corinne went on from a has-been to the third-biggest recording star in the world, and while this was important, what he remembered was that Polly, who had trouble with her size, ate all the bread and butter on the table during her mummy's first critical set and when this was finished—Farragut meant the set—everybody stood up and cheered and Polly grasped his arm and said: "That's my mummy, that's my dear mummy." So there was dear mummy in a hard spot that blazed with the blues of a diamond and would in fact prove to be the smile of the world and how could you square this with lullabys and breast-feeding except by eating opium? For Farragut the word "mother" evoked the image of a woman pumping gas, curtsying at the Assemblies and banging a lectern with her gavel. This confused him and he would blame his confusion on the fine arts, on Degas. There is a Degas painting of a woman with a bowl of chrysanthemums that had come to represent to Farragut the great serenity of "mother." The world kept urging him to match his own mother, a famous arsonist, snob, gas pumper and wing shot, against the image of the stranger with her autumnal and bitter-smelling flowers. Why had the universe encouraged this gap? Why had he been encouraged to cultivate so broad a border of sorrow? He had not been plucked off some star by a stork, so why should he and everybody else behave as if this were the case? The opium eater knew better. After Corinne's big comeback and breakthrough there was a big triumphant party and when he and Polly came in, dear Mummy made a straight line for her only daughter, her only child. "Polly," she said, "I could have *killed* you. You sat right in front of me, right in front of me, and during the first set of my big comeback you ate a whole basket of rolls—eight: I counted them—and you cleaned up one of those ice cream scoops of butter. How can I follow my arrangements when I'm counting the rolls you eat? Oh, I could have *killed* you." Polly, plucked from a star, began to weep, of course, and he got her out of there and back to the hotel, where they had some great Colombian cocaine that made their noses bleed. What else could you do? But Polly was thirty pounds overweight and he had never really liked fat women; he had never really liked any woman who wasn't a dark-eyed blonde, who didn't speak at least one language other than English, who didn't have an income of her own and who couldn't say the Girl Scout Oath.

Farragut's father, Farragut's own father, had wanted to have his life extinguished as he dwelt in his mother's womb, and how could he live happily with this knowledge without the support of those plants that draw their wisdom from the soil? Farragut's father had taken him fishing in the wilderness and had taught him to climb high mountains, but when he had discharged these responsibilities he neglected his son and spent most of his time tacking around Travertine harbor in a little catboat. He talked about having outmaneuvered great storms—a tempest off Falmouth was his favorite —but during Farragut's lifetime he preferred safe harbors. He was one of those old Yankees who are very adroit at handling their tiller and their sheets. He was great with all lines—kite lines, trout lines and moorings—and he could coil a garden hose with an authority that seemed to Farragut princely. Dance—excepting a German waltz with a pretty woman—the old man thought detestable, but dance best described his performance on a boat. The instant he dropped the mooring he began a performance as ordained, courtly and graceful as any pavane. Line squalls, luffing sails, thunder and lightning never broke his rhythm.

O heroin, be with me now! When Farragut was about twenty-one he began to lead the Nanuet Cotillion. The *Nanuet* landed in the New World in 1672. The leader of the expedition was Peter Wentworth. With his brother Eben away, Farragut was, after his drunken and cranky father, the principal male descendent of Wentworth, and so he led the cotillion. It had been a pleasure to leave the gas tanks to Harry—a spastic—and dress in his father's tails. This was again the thrill of living in a border principality and of course the origin of his opium eating. His father's tails fitted perfectly. They were made of black broadcloth, as heavy as the stuff of an overcoat, and Farragut thought he looked great in tails. He would drive into the city in whichever car was working, lead some debutante, chosen by the committee for her wealth and her connections, down to the principal box, and bow to its occupants. Then he would dance all night and get back to the gas pumps in the morning.

The Farraguts were the sort of people who claimed to be sustained by tradition, but who were in fact sustained by the much more robust pursuit of a workable improvisation, uninhibited by consistency. While they were still living in the mansion, they used to have dinner at the club on Thursdays and Sundays. Farragut remembered such a night. His mother had brought the car under the porte-cochere. The car was a convertible called a Jordan Blue Boy that his father had won in a raffle. His father wasn't with them and was probably on his catboat. Farragut got into the Blue Boy, but his brother remained on the carriage step. Eben was a handsome young man, but his face that night was very white. "I will not go to the club," he told his mother, "unless you call the steward by his name." "His name," said Mrs. Farragut, "is Horton." "His name is Mr. Horton," said Eben. "Very well," said Mrs. Farragut. Eben got into the car. Mrs. Farragut was not an intentionally reckless driver, but her vision was failing and on the road she was an agent of death. She had already

killed one Airedale and three cats. Both Eben and Farragut shut their eyes until they heard the sound of the
gravel on the club driveway. They took a table and
when the steward came to welcome them their mother
asked: "What are you going to tempt us with tonight,
Horton?" "Excuse me," said Eben. He left the table and
walked home. When Farragut returned he found his
brother—a grown man—sobbing in his room; but even
Eben, his only brother, had been inconsistent. Years
later, when they used to meet for drinks in New York,
Eben would summon the waiter by clapping his hands.
Once, after the headwaiter had asked them to leave
and Farragut had tried to explain to Eben that there
were simpler and more acceptable ways of getting a
waiter's attention, Eben had said, "I don't understand, I
simply don't understand. All I wanted was a drink."

Opium had helped Farragut recall with serenity the
fact that he had not been sixteen the first time his
father threatened to commit suicide. He was sure of his
age because he didn't have a driver's license. He came
in from pumping gas to find the supper table set for
two. "Where's Dad?" he asked—impetuously, because
the laconism cultivated by the Farraguts was cere-
monial and tribal and one seldom asked questions. His
mother sighed and served the red flannel hash with
poached eggs. Farragut had already faulted and so he
went on: "But where is Dad?" he asked. "I'm not sure,"
his mother said. "When I came downstairs to make
supper he handed me a long indictment enumerating
my failures as a woman, a wife and a mother. There
were twenty-two charges. I didn't read them all. I threw
it into the fire. He was quite indignant. He said that he

was going to Nagasakit and drown himself. He must
have begged rides since he didn't take the car." "Excuse
me," said Farragut, quite sincerely. No sarcasm was
intended. Some of the family must have said as much
as they lay dying. He got into the car and headed for
the beach. That's how he remembered that he was not
sixteen, because there was a new policeman in the
village of Hepworth, who was the only one who might
have stopped him and asked to see his license. The
policeman in Hepworth had it in for the family for
some reason. Farragut knew all the other policemen in
the villages along that coast.

When he got to Nagasakit he ran down to the
beach. It was late in the season, late in the day, and
there were no bathers, no lifeguards, nothing at all but
a very weary swell from what was already a polluted
ocean. How could he tell if it contained his father, with
pearls for eyes? He walked along the crescent of the
beach. The amusement park was still open. He could
hear some music from there, profoundly unserious and
belonging very much to the past. He examined the sand
to keep from crying. There had been that year a big run
on Japanese sandals and also a run on toy knights in
armor. There were, left over from the summer, many
dismembered knights and odd sandals mixed in the
shingle. Respiratory noises came from his beloved sea.
The roller coaster was still running. He could hear the
clack of the cars on the rail joints and also some very
loud laughter—a sound that seemed wasted on that
scene. He left the beach. He crossed the road to the
entrance of the amusement park. The façade marked a
period in the Italian emigration. Workmen from Italy

had built a wall of plaster and cement, painted it the saffrons of Rome, and decorated the wall with mermaids and scallop shells. Over the arch was Poseidon with a trident. On the other side of the wall the merry-go-round was turning. There was not a passenger on it. The loud laughter came from some people who were watching the roller coaster. There was Farragut's father, pretending to drink from an empty bottle and pretending to contemplate suicide from every rise. This clowning was successful. His audience was rapt. Farragut went up to the razorback who ran the controls. "That's my father," he said, "could you land him?" The smile the razorback gave Farragut was profoundly sympathetic. When the car carrying his father stopped at the platform, Mr. Farragut saw his son, his youngest, his unwanted, his killjoy. He got out and joined Farragut, as he knew he must. "Oh, Daddy," said Farragut, "you shouldn't do this to me in my formative years." Oh, Farragut, why is you an addict?

In the morning Tiny brought him four large tomatoes and he was touched. They tasted grievously of summer and freedom. "I'm going to sue," he told Tiny. "Can you get me a copy of Gilbert's criminal code?" "I can try," said Tiny. "Mishkin has one, but he's renting it out at four cartons a month. You got four?" "I can get them if my wife ever comes," said Farragut. "I'm going to sue, Tiny, but you're not whom I'm after. I want to see Chisholm and those other two assholes eating franks and beans for four years with a spoon. And maybe I can. Will you testify?" "Sure, sure," said Tiny. "I will if I can. I don't like the way Chisholm gets his kicks out of watching men in withdrawal. I'll do what I can." "The case seems very simple to me," said Farragut. "I was sentenced to prison by the people of the state and the nation. Medicine was prescribed for me, during my imprisonment, by three estimable members of the medical profession. This medicine was denied me by the deputy warden, a man employed by the people to supervise my penance. He then declared my predictable death throes to be an entertainment. It's that simple."

"Well, you can try," said Tiny. "Ten, fifteen years ago a fellow who got beat up sued and they gave him a lot of skin grafts. And when they knocked out Freddy the Killer's teeth he sued and they gave him two new sets of teeth. He never wore them except when we had turkey. Freddy was a great basketball star, but that was long before your time. Twenty-five, twenty-four years ago we had an undefeated basketball team here. I'm off tomorrow, but I'll see you the day after. Oh, Farragut, why is you an addict?"

When the bandages were taken off Farragut's skull, he found, of course, that his head had been shaven, but there were no mirrors around the infirmary and he didn't have his appearance to worry about. He tried with his fingers to count the stitches on his skull, but he could not keep an accurate count. He asked the orderly if he knew how many there were. "Oh, sure, sure," the orderly said. "You got twenty-two. I went to cellblock F to get you. You was lying on the floor. Tony and I got the stretcher and brought you up to the operating room." The fact that he, Farragut, had it in his power to send Chisholm, the deputy warden, to prison appeared to him as an unchallengeable fact. The image of the deputy warden eating franks and rice with a spoon appeared to him with the windless serenity of a consummated obsession. It was simply a question of time. His leg was in a cast, he had been told, because he had torn the cartilage in his knee. That he had twice before torn the cartilage in his knee in skiing accidents was something that he was absolutely incapable of remembering. He would limp for the rest of his life and he was profoundly gratified to think that the deputy warden had made an entertainment of his death throes and left him a cripple.

"Tell me again," Farragut asked the orderly. "How many stitches were there in my skull?" "Twenty-two, twenty-two," said the orderly. "I already told you. You bled like a pig. I know what I'm talking about because I used to kill pigs. When Tony and I went down to your cellblock there was blood all over the place. You was lying on the floor." "Who else was there?" asked Farragut. "Tiny, naturally," said the orderly. "Chisholm, the deputy warden, and Lieutenant Sutfin and Lieutenant Tillitson. Also there was a dude in cell lock. I don't know who he was." "Would you repeat what you've just said to a lawyer?" asked Farragut. "Sure, sure—it's what I saw. I'm a truthful man. I say what I see." "Could I see a lawyer?" "Sure, sure," said the orderly. "They come in once or twice a week. There's a Committee for the Legal Protection of Inmates. The next time one comes in I'll tell him about you."

A few days later a lawyer came over to Farragut's bed. His hair and his beard were so full that Farragut couldn't judge his age or his face, although there was no gray in his beard. His voice was light. His brown suit was worn, there was mud on his right shoe and two of his fingernails were dirty. The investment in his legal education had never been recouped. "Good morning," he said, "let's see, let's see. I'm sorry to be so slow, but I didn't know that you wanted the law until the day before yesterday." He carried a clipboard with a thick file of papers. "Here are your facts," he said. "I think I've got everything here. Armed robbery. Zip to ten. Second offense. That's you, isn't it?" "No," said Farragut. "Burglary?" the lawyer asked. "Breaking and entering with criminal intent?" "No," said Farragut. "Well, then, you must be second-degree homicide. Fratricide. You attempted escape on the eighteenth and you were disciplined. If you'll just sign this release here, no charges will be brought." "What kind of charges?" "Attempted escape," said the lawyer. "You can get seven years for that. But if you sign this release the whole thing will be forgotten." He passed Farragut the clipboard and a pen. Farragut held the board on his knees and the pen in his hand. "I didn't attempt escape," he said, "and I have witnesses. I was in the lower tier of cellblock F in the sixth lock-in of a maximum-security prison. I attempted to leave my cell, driven by the need for prescribed medicine. If an attempt to leave one's cell six lock-ins deep in a maximum-security prison constitutes an attempted escape, this prison is a house of cards."

"Oh, my," said the lawyer. "Why don't you reform the Department of Correction?"

"The Department of Correction," said Farragut, "is

merely an arm of the judiciary. It is not the warden and the assholes who sentenced us to prison. It is the judiciary."

"Oh ho ho," said the lawyer. "I have a terrible backache." He leaned forward stiffly and massaged his back with his right hand. "I got a backache from eating cheeseburgers. You got any home remedy for backaches contracted while eating cheeseburgers? Just sign the release and I'll leave you and your opinions alone. You know what they say about opinions?"

"Yes," said Farragut. "Opinions are like assholes. Everybody has one and they all smell."

"Oh ho ho," said the lawyer. His voice sounded very light and youthful. Farragut hid his pen under the bedclothes. "You know Charlie?" the lawyer asked, softly, softly. "I've seen him in chow," said Farragut. "I know who he is. I know that nobody speaks to him."

"Charlie's a great fellow," said the lawyer. "He used to work for Pennigrino, the top pimp. Charlie used to discipline the chicks." Now his voice was very low. "When a chick went wrong Charlie used to break her legs backwards. You want to play Scrabble with Charlie —you want to play Scrabble with Charlie or you want to sign this release?"

Farragut, with a swift, geometrical calculation of the possible charges involved, fired the clipboard at the beard. "Oh, my back," said the lawyer, "oh, God, my back." He got to his feet. He carried the clipboard. He put his right hand in his pocket. He did not seem to notice the loss of his pen. He did not speak to the orderly or the guards, but went straight out of the ward. Farragut began to insert the pen up his asshole.

From what he had been told—from what he had seen of the world—his asshole was singularly small, unreceptive and frigid. He got the pen in only as far as the clip and this was painful, but the pen was concealed. The orderly was called out of the ward and when he returned he went directly to Farragut and asked if he had the lawyer's pen. "I know I threw the clipboard at him," said Farragut. "I'm terribly sorry. I lost my temper. I hope I didn't hurt him."

"He said he left his pen here," said the orderly. He looked under the bed, in the drawer of the cabinet, under the pillow, along the window sill and under the mattress. Then a guard joined him in the search, stripped the bed, stripped Farragut naked and made some slighting reference to the size of his cock, but neither of them—through kindness, Farragut thought—went near the pen. "I can't find it," said the orderly. "We've got to find it," said the guard. "He says we've got to find it." "Well, tell him to find it himself," said the orderly. The guard went out and Farragut was afraid that the beard would return, but the guard returned alone and spoke to the orderly. "You're going up in the world," said the orderly to Farragut, very sadly. "They're putting you in a private room."

He passed Farragut his crutches and helped him into his shift. Farragut, swinging forward clumsily on his crutches and with the pen up his ass, followed the guard out of the ward and down a corridor that smelled sharply of quicklime to a door locked with a bar and a padlock. The guard had some trouble with the key. The door opened onto a very small cell with a window too high to be seen from, a toilet, a Bible and a mattress

with a folded sheet and blanket. "How long?" asked
Farragut. "The lawyer's booked you in for a month,"
said the guard, "but I seen Tiny give you some tomatoes
and if Tiny's your friend you'll be out in a week." He
shut and barred the door.

Farragut removed the pen. It was with this precious
instrument that he would indict Chisholm, and he
clearly saw Chisholm in his third year of prison grays
eating franks and rice with a bent tin spoon. He needed
paper. There was no toilet paper. If he demanded this
he would, he knew, with luck get one sheet a day. He
seized on the Bible. This was a small copy, bound in
red, but the end pages were a solid, clerical black and
the rest of the pages were so heavily printed that he
could not write over them. He wanted to write his
indictment of Chisholm at once. That the lawyer had
been determined to deny him a pen may have exaggerated the importance of his writing the indictment, but
the only alternative would be to phrase his accusation
and commit this to memory and he doubted if he could
accomplish this. He had the pen, but the only surface
upon which he could write seemed to be the wall of his
cell. He could write his indictment on the wall and then
commit it to memory, but some part of his background
and its influence on his character restrained him from
using the wall for a page. He was a man, he preserved
at least some vision of dignity, and to write what might
be his last statement on the wall seemed to him an
undue exploitation of a bizarre situation. His regard for
rectitude was still with him. He could write on his
plaster cast, his shift or his sheet. The plaster cast was
out since he could reach only half of its surface and the

roundness of the cast left him a very limited area. He wrote a few letters on his shift. The instant the felt pen touched the cloth, the ink spread to display the complexity of the thread count, the warp and woof of this very simple garment. The shift was out. His prejudice against the wall was still strong and so he tried the sheet. The prison laundry had, mercifully, used a great deal of starch and he found the surface of the sheet nearly as useful as paper. He and the sheet would be together for at least a week. He could cover the sheet with his remarks, clarify and edit these, and then commit them to memory. When he returned to cellblock F and the shop, he could type his remarks and have them kited to his governor, his bishop and his girl.

"Your Honor," he began. "I address you in your elective position from my elective position. You have been elected to the office of governor by a slender majority of the population. I have been elected to occupy cellblock F and to bear the number 734–508–32 by a much more ancient, exalted and unanimous force, the force of justice. I had, so to speak, no opponents. However, I am very much a citizen. As a taxpayer in the fifty percent bracket I have made a substantial contribution to the construction and maintenance of the walls that confine me. I have paid for the clothes I wear and the food I eat. I am a much more representative elected member of society than you. There are, in your career, broad traces of expedience, evasion, corruption and improvisation. The elective office that I hold is pure.

"We come, of course, from different classes. If intellectual and social legacies were revered in this country I would not consider addressing you, but we are dealing with a Democracy. I have never had the pleasure of your hospitality although I have twice been a guest at the White House as a delegate to conferences on higher education. I think the White House palatial. My quarters here are bare, seven by ten and dominated by a toilet that flushes capriciously anywhere from ten to forty times a day. It is easy for me to bear the sound of rushing water because I have heard the geysers in Yellowstone National Park, the fountains of Rome, New York City and especially Indianapolis.

"Sometime in April, twelve years ago, I was diagnosed as a chronic drug addict by Drs. Lemuel Brown, Rodney Coburn and Henry Mills. These men were graduates of Cornell, the Albany Medical School and Harvard University, respectively. Their position as healers was established by the state and the federal governments and the organizations of their colleagues. Surely, when they spoke, their expressed medical opinion was the voice of the commonwealth. On Thursday, the eighteenth of July, this unassailable opinion was contravened by Deputy Warden Chisholm. I have checked on Chisholm's background. Chisholm dropped out of high school in his junior year, bought the answers to a civil service test for correctional employees for twelve dollars and was given a position by the Department of Correction with monarchal dominion over my constitutional rights. At 9 A.M. on the morning of the eighteenth, Chisholm capriciously chose to overthrow the laws of the state, the federal government and the ethics of the medical profession, a profession that is surely a critical part of our social keystone. Chisholm decided to deny me the healing medicine that society had determined was my right. Is this not subversion, treachery, is this not high treason when the edicts of the Constitution are overthrown at the whim of one, single, uneducated man? Is this not an offense punishable by death—or in some states by life imprisonment? Is this not more far-reaching in its destructive precedents than some miscarried assassination attempt? Does it not strike more murderously at the heart of our hard-earned and ancient philosophy of government than rape or homicide?

"The rightness of the doctors' diagnoses was, of course, proven. The pain I suffered upon the withdrawal of that medicine granted to me by the highest authority in the land was mortal. When Deputy Warden Chisholm saw me attempt to leave my cell to go to the infirmary he tried to kill me with a chair. There are twenty-two sutures in my skull and I will be crippled for life. Are our institutions of penology, correction and rehabilitation to be excluded from the laws that mankind has considered to be just and urgently necessary to the continuation of life on this continent and indeed this planet? You may wonder what I am doing in prison and I will be very happy to inform you, but I thought it my duty to first inform you of the cancerous criminal treason that eats at the heart of your administration."

He scarcely paused between his letter to his governor and his letter to his bishop. "Your Grace," he wrote. "My name is Ezekiel Farragut and I was christened in Christ's Church at the age of six months. If proof is needed, my wife has a photograph of me taken, not that day, I think, but soon after. I am wearing a long lace gown that must have some history. My head is hairless and protuberant and looks like a darning egg. I am smiling. I was confirmed at the age of eleven by Bishop Evanston in the same church where I was christened. I have continued to take Holy Communion every Sunday of my life, barring those occasions when I was unable to find a church. In the provincial cities and towns of Europe I attend the Roman Mass. I am a croyant—I detest the use of French words in English, but in this case I can think of nothing better—and as croyants I'm sure we share the knowledge that to profess exalted religious experience outside the ecclesiastical paradigm is to make of oneself an outcast; and by that I mean to hear the cruel laughter of those men and women to whom we look for love and mercy; I mean the pain of fire and ice; I mean the desolation of being buried at a crossroads with a stake through one's heart. I truly believe in One God the Father Almighty but I know that to say so loudly, and at any distance from the chancel —any distance at all—would dangerously jeopardize my ability to ingratiate those men and women with whom I wish to live. I am trying to say—and I'm sure you will agree with me—that while we are available to transcendent experience, we can state this only at the suitable and ordained time and in the suitable and ordained place. I could not live without this knowledge; no more could I live without the thrilling possibility of suddenly encountering the fragrance of skepticism.

"I am a prisoner. My life follows very closely the traditional lives of the saints, but I seem to have been forgotten by the blessed company of all faithful men and women. I have prayed for kings, presidents and bishops, but I have never once said a prayer for a man in prison nor have I ever heard a hymn that mentioned jail. We prisoners, more than any men, have suffered for our sins, we have suffered for the sins of society, and our example should cleanse the thoughts of men's hearts because of the grief with which we are acquainted. We are in fact the word made flesh; but what I want to do is to call your attention to a great blasphemy.

"As Your Grace well knows, the most universal image of mankind is not love or death; it is Judgment Day. One sees this in the cave paintings in the Dordogne, in the tombs of Egypt, in the temples of Asia and Byzantium, in Renaissance Europe, England, Russia and the Golden Horn. Here the Divinity sifts out the souls of men, granting to the truly pure infinite serenity and sentencing the sinners to fire, ice and sometimes piss and shit. Social custom is never in force where one finds this vision, and one finds it everywhere. Even in Egypt the candidates for immortality include souls who could be bought and sold in the world of the living. The Divinity is the flame, the heart of this vision. A queue approaches the Divinity, always from the right; it doesn't matter what country, age or century from which the vision is reported. On the left, then, one sees the forfeits and the rewards. Forfeiture and torment are, even in the earliest reports, much more passionately painted than eternal peace. Men thirsted, burned and took it up the ass with much more force and passion than they played their harps and flew. The presence of God binds the world together. His force, His essence, is Judgment.

"Everyone knows that the only sacraments are bread and water. The hymeneal veil and the golden ring came in only yesterday, and as an incarnation of the vision of love, Holy Matrimony is only a taste of the hellish consequences involved in claiming that a vision can be represented by thought, word and deed. Here, in my cell, is what one sees in the caves, the tombs of the kings, the temples and churches all over the planet being performed by men, by any kind of men the last century might have bred. Stars, dumbbells, hacks and boobs—it is they who have constructed these caverns of hell and, with a familiar diminishment of passion, the fields of paradise on the other side of the wall. This is the obscenity, this is the unspeakable obscenity, this stupid pageantry of judgment that, finer than air or gas, fills these cells with the reek of men slaughtering one another for no real reason to speak of. Denounce this cardinal blasphemy, Your Grace, from the back of your broad-winged eagle."

"Oh, my darling," he wrote, with no pause at all and to a girl he had lived with for two months when Marcia had abdicated and moved to Carmel. "Last night, watching a comedy on TV, I saw a woman touch a man with familiarity—a light touch on the shoulder—and I lay on my bed and cried. No one saw me. Prisoners, of course, suffer a loss of identity, but this light touch gave me a terrifying insight into the depth of my alienation. Excepting myself there is truly no one here with whom I can speak. Excepting myself there is nothing I can touch that is warm, human and responsive. My reason with its great claims to strength, light and usefulness is totally crippled without the warmth of sentiment. An obscene nothing is forced onto me. I do not love, I am unloved, and I can only remember the raptness of love faintly, faintly. If I close my eyes and try to pray I will fall into the torpor of solitude. I will try to remember.

"In remembering, my darling, I will try to avoid mentioning specific fucks or places or clothes or feats of mutual understanding. I can remember coming back to the Danieli on the Lido after a great day on the beach when we had both been solicited by practically everybody. It was at that hour when the terrible, the uniquely terrible band began to play terrible, terrible tangos and the beauties of the evening, the girls and boys in their handmade clothes, had begun to emerge. I can remember this but I don't choose to. The landscapes that come to my mind are unpleasantly close to what one finds on greeting cards—the snowbound farmhouse is recurrent—but I would like to settle for something inconclusive. It is late in the day. We have spent the day on a beach. I can tell because we are burned from the sun and there is sand in my shoes. A taxi—some hired livery—has brought us to a provincial railroad station, an isolated place, and left us there. The station is locked and there is no town, no farmhouse, no sign of life around the place excepting a stray dog. When I look at the timetable nailed to the station house I realize that we are in Italy although I don't know where. I've chosen this memory because there are few specifics. We have either missed the train or there is no train or the train is late. I don't remember. I can't even remember laughter or a kiss or putting my arm around your shoulder as we sat on a hard bench in an empty provincial railroad station in some country where English was not spoken. The light was going, but going, as it so often does, with a fanfare. All I really remember is a sense of your company and a sense of physical contentment.

"I suppose I am dealing with romantic and erotic things, but I think I am dealing with much more. What I remember, tonight in this cell, is waiting in some living room for you to finish dressing. I hear the sound from the bedroom of you closing a drawer. I hear the sound of your heels—the floor, the carpet, the tile of the bathroom—as you go there to flush the toilet. Then I hear the sound of your heels again—a little swifter now—as you open and close another drawer and then come toward the door of the room where I wait, bringing with you the pleasures of the evening and the night and the life we have together. And I can remember wishing for dinner in an upstairs bedroom while you did the last thing before putting dinner on the table, while I heard you touch a china serving dish with a pot. That is what I remember.

"And I remember when we first met, and I am today and will be forever astonished at the perspicacity with which a man can, in a glimpse, judge the scope and beauty of a woman's memory, her tastes in color, food, climate and language, the precise clinical dimensions of her visceral, cranial and reproductive tracts, the condition of her teeth, hair, skin, toenails, eyesight and bronchial tree, that he can, in a second, exalted by the diagnostics of love, seize on the fact that she is meant for him or that they are meant for one another. I am speaking of a glimpse and the image seems to be transitory, although this is not so much romantic as it is practical since I am thinking of a stranger, seen by a stranger. There will be stairs, turnings, gangplanks, elevators, seaports, airports, someplace between somewhere and somewhere else and where I first saw you wearing blue and reaching for a passport or a cigarette. Then I pursued you across the street, across the country and around the world, absolutely and rightly informed of the fact that we belonged in one another's arms as we did.

"You are not the most beautiful woman I have ever known, but four of the great beauties I have known died by their own hand and while this does not mean that all the great beauties I have known have killed themselves, four is a number to consider. I may be trying to explain the fact that while your beauty is not great, it is very practical. You have no nostalgia. I think nostalgia a primary female characteristic and you have it not at all. You have a marked lack of sentimental profoundness, but you have a brightness, a quality of light, that I have never seen equaled. Everyone knows this, everyone sees this, everyone responds. I can't imagine this being eclipsed. Your physical coordination in athletics can be very depressing. You have to throw me a tennis game and you can even beat me at horseshoes, but what I remember is that you were never aggressive. I remember fishing with you in Ireland. Remember? We stayed in that beautiful manor with an international crowd including several German barons with monocles. Maids with caps served tea. Remember? My gillie was sick that day and we went up the stream alone—it was called the Dillon—to a bend where there was a little sign that said you couldn't take more than one large salmon a day out of the pool. Above the bend in the stream there was a hill and on the hill there was a ruined castle with a big tree sticking out of the highest tower and in the ruin of the great hall swarms and swarms of bumblebees taking the nectar out of a vine that was covered with white flowers. We didn't go into the manor hall because we didn't want to get stung, but I remember walking away from the castle and smelling the heavy scent of the white flowers and the loud, loud noise the bees made— it was like the drone of some old-fashioned engine with a leather traveling belt—and it reached all the way down the hill to the edge of the stream and I remember looking at the greenness of the hills and your brightness and the romantic ruin and hearing the drone of the bees and tying my leader and thanking God that this hadn't happened to me earlier in life because it would have been the end. I mean I would have become one of those jugheads who sit around cafés with faraway looks in their eyes because they have heard the music of the spheres. So I placed my line, knowing all the time that with your coordination you could place a line much better than I, while you sat on the banks with your hands folded in your lap as if you wished you had brought your embroidery although you can't, so far as I know, sew on a button. So then I hooked and landed a big salmon and then there was a thunderstorm and we got soaked and then we stripped and swam in the stream, which was warmer than the rain, and then they served the salmon that night at the manor with a lemon in its mouth but what I intended to say is that you weren't aggressive and as I recall we never quarreled. I remember once looking at you in some hotel room and thinking that if I love her so absolutely we must quarrel and if I didn't dare to quarrel perhaps I didn't dare to love. But I loved you and we didn't quarrel and I can't ever remember our quarreling, never, never, not even when I was about to shoot all my guns and you took your tongue out of my mouth and said that I still hadn't told you whether you should wear a long dress or a short dress to the Pinhams' birthday party. Never.

"And I remember some mountainous place in the winter on the eve of a holiday where thousands of people had gathered to ski and where thousands more were expected on the late planes and trains. And I remember ski places, those overheated rooms and the books that people leave behind them and the galvanic excitement of physicalness. We were in bed then, when there was, around midnight, a sudden rise in temperature. The thawing snow on the roof made a dripping sound—a water torture for the innkeeper and killjoy music for everyone else. So in the morning it was very warm by whatever standards or measures used in whatever country it was. The snow was sticky enough for snowballs and I formed one and fired it at a tree, hitting or missing I don't remember, but beyond the snowball we saw the warm blue sky and the snow melting everywhere. But it would be colder on the mountains whose white slopes and summits surrounded us. We took the funicular up, but even on the summit the snow was warm, the day was disastrous, spiritually, financially, we were the prisoners of our environment although if we had enough money we could have flown to some other, colder part of the world. Even on the summit of the mountain the snow was sticky, the day was like spring, and I skied half-naked, but the wet trails were perilous, swift in the shade, retarded in the sun, and in lower altitudes there was an inch of water in every declivity. Then at about eleven the wind changed and I had to get back into my underwear, my shirt, whatever else I had, and just as suddenly the trails turned to ice and one by one the rangers put up the CLOSED signs in seven languages at the beginnings of the trails and there was first the rumor and then the fact that the Italian prime minister had been killed taking a last run down the Gloken-schuss. Then no one was coming up the lift, there was a line waiting to descend, and while the lower trails were still not frozen and were negotiable that day, that holiday, that climax of the year was ruined. But then, exactly as the sun reached the zenith, snow began to fall. It was a very heavy and beautiful snow that, like some juxtaposition of gravity, seemed to set the mountain range free of the planet. We drank some coffee or schnapps in a hut—waited twenty minutes or half an hour—and then there was perfect cover on the lower trails and after an hour there was perfect cover every-where, perhaps four inches that fanned like spume when we turned, a gift, an epiphany, an unaccountable improvement on our mastery of those snow-buried slopes and falls. Then we went up and down, up and down, our strength inexhaustible, our turns snug and accomplished. The clinicians would say that we were skiing down every slope of our lives back to the instant of our birth; and men of good will and common sense would claim that we were skiing in every possible direction toward some understanding of the triumph of our beginnings and our ends. So when you ski you walk on beaches, you swim, you sail, you carry the groceries up the steps to a lighted house, you drop your pants on a large anatomical incongruity, you kiss a rose. We skied that day—those slopes were unlighted—until the valley telephoned the summit to close the lifts and then, reestablishing our terrestrial equilibrium as one does after a long sail, a hockey game—as tightrope artists must—we swaggered into the bar, where our cups and everything else were brimming. I can remember this and I can remember the sailboat race too, but it is getting dark here now, it is too dark for me to write anymore."

Farragut was still limping, but his hair had begun to grow back, when he was asked to cut a ditto sheet for an announcement that read: THE FIDUCIARY UNIVERSITY OF BANKING WILL OFFER A COURSE IN THE ESSENCE OF BANKING FOR ANY QUALIFIED INMATE. SEE YOUR CELLBLOCK OFFICER FOR FURTHER INFORMATION. That night Farragut asked Tiny about the news. Tiny told him that the class was going to be limited to thirty-six. Classes would be on Tuesdays and Thursdays. Anyone could apply, but the class would be chosen on the strength of an intelligence quotient test furnished by the university. That's all Tiny knew.

Toledo mimeographed the announcement and they were stuck into the cells along with the evening mail. Toledo should have mimeographed two thousand, but he seemed to have run off another two thousand because the fliers were all over the place. Farragut couldn't figure out where they came from, but when a wind sprang up in the yard you could see the Fiduciary University announcements circling on the air, not by the tens but by the hundreds. A few days after the announcements were circulated, Farragut had to ditto an announcement for the bulletin board. ANY MAN FOUND USING FIDUCIARY UNIVERSITY ANNOUNCEMENT FOR TOILET PAPER WILL BE GIVEN THREE DAYS CELL LOCK. THEY CLOG THE PLUMBING. Paper was always in short supply and this snow of fliers was a bounty. They were used for handkerchiefs, airplanes and scrap paper. The jailhouse lawyers used them for drafting petitions to the Pope, the President, the governor, the Congress and the Legal Aid Society. They were used for poems, prayers and illustrated solicitations. The greenhouse crew picked them up with nailed sticks, but for some time the flow of fliers seemed mysterious and inexhaustible.

This was in the autumn, and mixed with the Fiduciary University announcements were the autumn leaves. The three swamp maples within the wall had turned red and dropped their leaves early in the fall, but there were many trees beyond the wall and among the Fiduciary announcements Farragut saw the leaves of beech trees, oaks, tulips, ash, walnut and many varieties of maple. The leaves had the power to remind

Farragut, an hour or so after methadone, of the enormous and absurd pleasure he had, as a free man, taken in his environment. He liked to walk on the earth, swim in the oceans, climb the mountains and, in the autumn, watch the leaves fall. The simple phenomenon of light —brightness angling across the air—struck him as a transcendent piece of good news. He thought it fortunate that as the leaves fell, they turned and spun, presenting an illusion of facets to the light. He could remember a trustees meeting in the city over a matter of several million dollars. The meeting was on the lower floor of a new office building. Some ginkgo trees had been planted in the street. The meeting was in October when the ginkgos turn a strikingly pure and uniform yellow, and during the meeting he had, while watching these leaves fall across the air, found his vitality and his intelligence suddenly stimulated and had been able to make a substantial contribution to the meeting founded foursquare on the brightness of leaves.

Above the leaves and the fliers and the walls were the birds. Farragut was a little wary about the birds since the legend of cruelly confined men loving the birds of the air had never moved him. He tried to bring a practical and informed tone to his interest in birds, but he had very little information. He became interested in a flock of red-winged blackbirds. They lived in swamps, he knew, so there must have been a swamp near Falconer. They fed at dusk in some stagnant water other than the swamp where they lived. Night after night, all through the summer and deep into the fall, Farragut stood at his window and watched the black birds cross the blue sky above the walls. There would be one or two in the beginning, and while they must have been leaders, there was nothing adventurous about their flight. They all had the choppy flight of caged birds. After the leaders came a flock of two or three hundred, all of them flying clumsily but given by their numbers a sense of power—the magnetic stamina of the planet—drawn through the air like embers on a strong draft. After the first flock there were more laggards, more adventurers, and then another flock of hundreds or thousands and then a third. They made their trip back to their home in the swamp after dark and Farragut could not see this. He stood at the window waiting to hear the sound of their passage, but it never happened. So in the autumn he watched the birds, the leaves and the Fiduciary University announcements moving as the air moved, like dust, like pollen, like ashes, like any sign of the invincible potency of nature.

Only five men in cellblock F applied for the course in banking. Nobody much took it seriously. They guessed that the Fiduciary University was either newborn or on the skids and had resorted to Falconer for publicity. The bounteous education of unfortunate convicts was always good for some space in the paper. When the time came, Farragut and the others went down to the parole board room to take the intelligence quotient test. Farragut knew that he tested badly. He had never tested over 119 and had once gone as low as 101. In the army this had kept him from any position of command and had saved his life. He took the test with twenty-four other men, counting blocks and racking his memory for the hypotenuse of the isosceles triangle. The scores were supposed to be secret, but for a package of cigarettes Tiny told him he had flunked out with 112. Jody scored at 140 and claimed he had never done so badly.

Jody was Farragut's best friend. They had met in the shower, where Farragut had noticed a slight young man with black hair smiling at him. He wore around his neck a simple and elegant gold cross. They were not allowed to speak in the shower, but the stranger, soaping his left shoulder, spread out his palm so that Farragut could read there, written in indelible ink: "Meet me later." When they had dressed they met at the door. "You the professor?" the stranger asked. "I'm 734–508–32," said Farragut. He was that green. "Well, I'm Jody," said the stranger brightly, "and I know you're Farragut but so long as you ain't homosexual I don't care what your name is. Come on with me. I'll show you my hideout." Farragut followed him across the grounds to an abandoned water tower. They climbed up a rusty ladder to a wooden catwalk where there was a mattress, a butt can and some old magazines. "Everybody's got to have a hideout," said Jody. "This is mine. The view is what they call the Millionaire's View. Next to the death house, this is the best place for seeing it." Farragut saw, over the roofs of the old cellblocks and the walls, a two-mile stretch of river with cliffs and mountains on the western shore. He had seen or glimpsed the view before at the foot of the prison street, but this was the most commanding sight he had been given of the world beyond the wall and he was deeply moved.

"Sit down, sit down," his friend said, "sit down and I'll tell you about my past. I ain't like most of the dudes, who won't tell you nothing. Everybody knows that Freddy, the Mad Dog Killer, iced six men, but you ask him, he'll tell you he's in for stealing flowers from some park. He ain't kidding. He means it. He really believes it. But when I have a buddy I tell him everything if he wants to hear it. I talk a lot, but I listen a lot too. I'm a very good listener. But my past is really my past. I don't have no future at all. I don't see the parole board for twelve years. What I do around here don't matter much, but I like to stay out of the hole. I know there ain't no medical evidence for brain damage, but after you hit yourself about fourteen times you get silly. Once I banged myself seven times. There wasn't nothing more to come out, but I went on banging myself. I couldn't stop. I was going crazy. That ain't healthy. Anyhow, I was indicted on fifty-three counts. I had a forty-five-thousand-dollar house in Leavittown, a great wife and two great sons: Michael and Dale. But I was in this bind. People with your kind of life style don't ever understand. I didn't graduate from high school, but I was up for an office in the mortgage department of Hamilton Trust. But nothing was moving. Of course, my not having an education was a drawback and they were laying people off, left and right. I just couldn't make enough money to support four people and when I put the house up for sale I discover that every fucking house on the block is on the market. I thought about money all the time. I dreamed about money. I was picking dimes, nickels and pennies off the sidewalk. I was bananas about money. So I had a friend named Howie and he had this solution. He told me about this old guy—Masterman—who ran a stationery store in the shopping center. He had two seven-thousand-dollar pari-mutuel tickets. He kept them in a drawer beside his bed. Howie knew this because he used to let the old man blow him for a fin. Howie had this wife, kids, a wood-burning fireplace, but no money. So we decided to get the tickets. In those days you didn't have to endorse them. It was fourteen thousand in cash and no way to trace it. So we watched the old man for a couple of nights. It was easy. He closed up the store at eight, drove home, got drunk, ate something and watched TV. So one night when he closed the store and got into his car we got into it with him. He was very obedient because I was holding this loaded gun against his head. This gun was Howie's. He drove home and we lock-stepped him up to the front door, poking the gun into any soft part of him that was convenient. We marched him into the kitchen and handcuffed him to this big Goddamned refrigerator. It was very big, a very recent model. We asked him where the tickets was and he said they was in the lockbox. If we pistol-whipped him like he said we did, it wasn't me. It could have been Howie, but I didn't see it. He kept telling us the two tickets was in the bank. So then we turned the house upside down looking for tickets, but I guess he was right. So we turned on the TV for neighbors and left him chained to this ten-ton refrigerator and took off in his car. The first car we saw was a police car. This was just an accident, but we got scared. We drove his car into one of those car washes where you have to get out of the car when it hits the shower. We put the car in the slot and took off. We got a bus into Manhattan and said goodbye at the terminal.

"But you know what that old sonofabitch Masterman did? He ain't big and he ain't strong, but he starts inching this big, fucking refrigerator across the kitchen floor. Believe me, it was enormous. It was really a nice house with lovely furniture and carpets and he must have had one hell of a time with all those carpets bunching up under the refrigerator, but he got out of the kitchen and down the hall and into the living room, where the telephone was. I can imagine what the police saw when they got there: this old man chained to a refrigerator in the middle of his living room with hand-painted pictures all over the walls. That was Thursday. They picked me up the following Tuesday. They already had Howie. I didn't know it, but he already had a record. I don't blame the state. I don't blame nobody. We did everything wrong. Burglary, pistol-whipping, kidnapping. Kidnapping's a big no-no. Of course, I'm the next thing to dead, but my wife and sons are still alive. So she sold the house at a big loss and goes on welfare. She comes to see me once in a while, but you know what the boys do? First they got permission to write me letters and then Michael, the big one, wrote me a letter saying that they would be on the river in a rowboat at three on Sunday and they would wave to me. I was out at the fence at three on Sunday and they showed up. They were way out in the river—you can't come too close to the prison—but I could see them and feel my love for them and they waved their arms and I waved my arms. That was in the autumn and they stopped coming when the place where you rent boats shut down, but they started again in the spring. They were much bigger, I could see that, and then it occurs to me that for the length of time I'm here they'll get married and have children and I know they won't stuff their wives or their kids into no rowboat and go down the river to wave to old Daddy. So I ain't got no future, Farragut, and you ain't got no future either. So let's go down and wash up for chow."

Farragut was working then part-time with the greenhouse crew, cutting lawns and hedges, and part-time as a typist, cutting ditto sheets for the prison announcements. He had the key to an office near the squad room and the use of a typewriter. He continued to meet Jody at the water tower and later, when the afternoons got cold, in his office. They had known one another a month when they became lovers. "I'm so glad you ain't homosexual," Jody kept saying when he caressed Farragut's hair. Then, saying as much one afternoon, he had unfastened Farragut's trousers and, with every assistance from Farragut, got them down around his knees. From what Farragut had read in the newspapers about prison life he had expected this to happen, but what he had not expected was that this grotesque bonding of their relationship would provoke in him so profound a love. Nor had he expected the administration to be so lenient. For a small ration of cigarettes, Tiny let Farragut return to the shop between chow and lockup. Jody met him there and they made love on the floor. "They like it," Jody explained. "At first they didn't like it. Then some psychologist decided that if we got our rocks moved regularly we wouldn't riot. They'll let us do anything if they think it will keep us from rioting. Move over, Chicken, move over. Oh, I love you very much."

They met two or three times a week. Jody was the beloved and now and then he stood Farragut up so that Farragut had developed a preternatural sensitivity to the squeak of his lover's basketball sneakers. On some nights his life seemed to hang on the sound. When the classes in banking began, the two men met always on Tuesdays and Thursdays and Jody reported on his experience with the university. Farragut had boosted a mattress from the shop and Jody had hustled a hot plate from somewhere, and they lay on the mattress and drank hot coffee and were fairly comfortable and happy.

But Jody spoke skeptically to Farragut about the university. "It's the same old shit," said Jody. "Success School. Charm School. Elite School. How to Make a Million School. I been to them all and they're all the same. You see, Chicken, banking arithmetic and all that shit is done by computers today and what you have to concentrate on is to inspire the confidence of the potential investor. That's the big mystery of modern banking. For instance, you come on with the smile. Every class I took begins with lessons in this smile. You stand outside the door thinking about all the great things that happened to you that day, that year, for your whole life. It has to be real. You can't fake this selling smile. I mean you remember a great girl who made you happy or winning a long shot if you ever had one or a new suit or a race you won or a great day when you really had everything going for you. Well, then you open the door and go in and smack him with this smile. Only they don't know nothing, Chicken. I mean about smiling. They don't know nothing at all about smiling.

"It's all right to smile, I mean you have to smile to sell anything, but if you don't smile in the right way you get terrible lines on your face like you have. I love you, Chicken, but you don't know how to smile. If you knew how to smile you wouldn't have those wrinkles all around your eyes and those big, disgusting cuts like scars on your face. Look at me, for example. You think I'm twenty-four, don't you? Well, I'm actually thirty-two, but most people when they're asked to guess my age put me down for eighteen or nineteen at the most. That's because I know how to smile, how to use my face. This actor taught me. He was in on a morals charge but he was very beautiful. He taught me that when you use your face you spare your face. When you throw your face recklessly into every situation you come up against, you come out looking like *you* do, you come out looking like shit. I love you, Chicken, I really do, otherwise I wouldn't tell you that you got a ruined face. Now watch me smile. See? I look real happy—don't I, don't I, don't I?—but if you'll notice, I keep my eyes wide open so I won't get disgusting wrinkles all around the edges like you have and when I open my mouth I open it very, very wide so that it won't destroy the beauty of my cheeks, their beauty and smoothness.

This teacher from the university tells us to smile, smile, smile, smile, but you go around smiling all the time like he teaches us to, you get to look like a very old person, a very old and haggard person who nobody wants anything to do with especially in the line of banking investments."

When Jody talked scornfully about the Fiduciary University, Farragut's attitude seemed parental, seemed to express some abiding respect for anything that was taught by an organization, however false the teaching and however benighted the organization. Listening to Jody describe the Fiduciary University as shit made Farragut wonder if disrespect was not at the bottom of Jody's criminal career and his life in prison. He felt that Jody should bring more patience, more intelligence, to his attacks on the university. It may have been no more than the fact that the word "fiduciary" seemed to him to deserve respect and inspire honesty; and in its train were thrift, industry, frugality and honest strife.

In fact, Jody's attacks on the university were continuous, predictable and, in the end, monotonous. Everything about the school was wrong. The teacher was ruining his face with too broad and committed a smile. The spot quizzes were too easy. "I don't do no work," Jody said, "and I always get the highest marks in the class. I got this memory. It's easy for me to remember things. I learned the whole catechism in one night. Now, today we had Nostalgia. You think it's got something to do with your nose. It don't. It's what you remember with pleasure. So what you do is your homework on what the potential investor remembers with pleasure and you play on his pleasant memories like a fucking violin. You not only stir up what they call Nostalgia with talk, you wear clothes and look and talk and use body language like something they're going to remember with pleasure. So the potential investor likes history, and can't you see me coming into the bank in a fucking suit of armor?"

"You're not taking it seriously, Jody," Farragut said. "There must be something worthwhile in it. I think you ought to pay more attention to what is useful in the course."

"Well, there may be something in it," Jody said. "But you see, I had it all before in Charm School, Success School, Elite School. It's all the same shit. I had it ten times before. Now, they tell me a man's name is for him the sweetest sound in the language. I know this, when I was three, four years old. I know the whole thing. You want to hear it? Listen."

Jody ticked off his points on the bars of Farragut's cell. "One. Let the other fellow feel that all the good ideas are his. Two. Throw down a challenge. Three. Open up with praise and honest appreciation. Four. If you're wrong admit it quickly. Five. Get the other person saying yes. Six. Talk about your mistakes. Seven. Let the other man save his face. Eight. Use encouragement. Nine. Make the thing you want to do seem easy. Ten. Make the other person seem happy about doing what you want. Shit, man, any hustler knows that. That's my life, that's the story of my life. I've been doing all this ever since I was a little kid and look where it got me. Look where my knowledge of the essence of charm and success and banking dumped me. Shit, Chicken, I feel like quitting."

"Don't, Jody," said Farragut. "Stay with it. You'll graduate and it'll look good on your record."

"Nobody's going to look at my record for another forty years," said Jody.

He came one night. It was snowing. "Put in for sick call tomorrow," Jody said. "Monday. There'll be a crowd. I'll wait for you outside the infirmary." He was gone. "Don't he love you no more?" asked Tiny. "Well, if he don't love you no more it's a weight off my shoulders. You're really a nice guy, Farragut. I like you, but I got no use for him. He's blown half the population and he's hardly begun. Last week, the week before last—I can't remember—he did this fan dance on the third tier. Toledo told me about it. He had this piece of newspaper pleated, you know, like a fan and he kept switching it from his cock to his asshole and doing this dance. Toledo said it was very disgusting. Very disgusting." Farragut tried to imagine this and couldn't. What he felt was that Tiny was jealous. Tiny had never experienced the love of a man. Tiny was insecure. He made out his sick-call slip, put it between the bars and went to bed.

The waiting room at the infirmary was full and he and Jody stood outside where no one could hear them. "Now, listen," Jody said. "Now, before you get upset listen to me. Don't say nothing until I stop talking. I quit the university yesterday. Now, don't say nothing. I know you're not going to like it because you got this father image thing about me being a big success in the

world, but wait until I tell you my plan. Don't say anything. I said don't say anything. Graduation is planned.
Nobody but us in the school knows what's going to
happen, but you will in a few days. Listen to this. The
cardinal, the cardinal of the diocese, is going to come
here in a helicopter and present the diplomas to the
graduating class. I'm not shitting you and don't ask me
why. I guess the cardinal's some kind of a relation to
somebody in the university, but it'll be great publicity
and that's what's going to happen. Now, one of the
dudes in the class is the chaplain's assistant. His name
is DiMatteo. He's a very close friend to me. So he's in
charge of all those dresses they wear on the altar, you
know. So what he's got is a red one, in my size, a
perfect fit. He's going to give it to me. So when the
cardinal comes there'll be a lot of confusion. So I'll
hang back, hide in the boiler room, get into my red
dress, and when the cardinal celebrates mass I'll get
my ass on the altar. Listen. I know what I'm doing. I
know. I served on the altar beginning when I was
eleven. That was when I was confirmed. I know you
think they'll catch me, but they won't. At mass you
don't look at the other acolytes. That's the thing about
prayer. You don't look. When you see a stranger on the
altar you don't go around asking who's the stranger on
the altar. This is holy business and when you're doing
holy business you don't see nothing. When you drink
the blood of Our Savior you don't look to see if the
chalice is tarnished or if there's bugs in the wine. You
get to be transfixed, you're like transfixed. Prayer.
That's why it is. Prayer is what's going to get me out of
this place. The power of prayer. So when the mass is

over I'll get in the helicopter in my red dress and if they ask me where I'm from I'll say I'm from Saint Anselm's, Saint Augustine's, Saint Michael's, Saint Anywheres. When we land I'll get out of my robes in the vestry and walk out on the street. What a miracle! I'll panhandle subway fare up to 174th Street, where I got friends. I'm telling you this, Chicken, because I love and trust you. I'm putting my life in your hands. Greater love hath no man. But don't expect to see very much of me from now on. This dude with the red dress likes me. The chaplain brings him in food from the outside and so I'm taking the electric plate. I may never see you again, Chicken, but if I can I'll come back and say goodbye." Jody then put his hands on his stomach, stooped and, groaning softly with pain, went into the waiting room. Farragut followed, but they didn't speak again. Farragut complained of headaches and the doctor gave him an aspirin. The doctor wore dirty clothes and had a large hole in his right sock.

Jody didn't return and Farragut missed him painfully. He listened through all the million sounds of the prison for the squeak of basketball sneakers. It was all he wanted to hear. Soon after their parting at the infirmary he was given the ditto sheet to type announcing that His Eminence Cardinal Thaddeus Morgan would arrive at Falconer by helicopter on the twenty-seventh of May to present diplomas to the graduating class of the Fiduciary University. He would be assisted by the governor and the commissioner of correction. Mass would be celebrated. Attendance at the ceremony would be mandatory and cellblock officers would have further information.

Toledo mimeographed the ditto but he didn't overdo it this time and there was no blizzard of paper. In the beginning the announcement had almost no impact at all. Only eight men were going to be graduated. The thought of Christ's Advocate descending from heaven onto the gallows field seemed to excite no one. Farragut, of course, went on listening for the squeak of basketball sneakers. If Jody came to say goodbye it would probably be the night before the cardinal's arrival. That gave Farragut a month of waiting to see his lover and then for only a moment. He had to settle for this. Jody, he guessed, was thrashing around with the chaplain's dude, but he did not experience any real jealousy. He could not honestly guess at whether or not Jody's plans to escape would succeed since both the cardinal's and Jody's plans were preposterous, although the cardinal's plans were reported in the newspaper.

Farragut lay on his cot. He wanted Jody. The longing began in his speechless genitals, for which his brain cells acted as interpreter. The longing then moved up from his genitals to his viscera and from there to his heart, his soul, his mind, until his entire carcass was filled with longing. He waited for the squeak of basketball sneakers and then the voice, youthful, calculatedly so perhaps, but not too light, asking: Move over, Chicken. He waited for the squeak of basketball sneakers as he had waited for the sound of Jane's heels on the cobbles in Boston, waited for the sound of the elevator that would bring Virginia up to the eleventh floor, waited for Dodie to open the rusty gate on Thrace Street, waited for Roberta to get off the C bus in some Roman piazza, waited for Lucy to install her diaphragm and appear naked in the bathroom door, waited for telephone bells, doorbells, church bells that told the time, waited for the end of the thunderstorm that was frightening Helen, waited for the bus, the boat, the train, the plane, the hydrofoil, the helicopter, the ski lift, the five o'clock whistle and the fire alarm to deliver his beloved into his arms. It seemed that he had spent an inordinate amount of his life and his energies waiting, but that waiting was not, even when no one came, an absolute frustration; it took some of its nature from the grain of the vortex.

But why did he long so for Jody when he had often thought that it was his role in life to possess the most beautiful women? Women possessed the greatest and the most rewarding mysteriousness. They were approached in darkness and sometimes, but not always, possessed in darkness. They were an essence, fortified and besieged, worth conquering and, once conquered, flowing with spoils. At his horniest he wanted to reproduce, to populate hamlets, towns, villages and cities. It seemed to be his desire to fructify that drove him to imagine fifty women quickening with his children. Women were Ali Baba's cave, they were the light of the morning, they were waterfalls, thunderstorms, they were the immensities of the planet, and a vision of this had led him to decide on something better when he rolled naked off his last naked scoutmaster. There was a trace of reproach in his memory of their splendor, but reproach was not what he meant. Considering the sovereignty of his unruly cock, it was only a woman who could crown that redness with purpose.

There was, he thought, some sameness of degree in

sexual possession and sexual jealousy; and accommodations and falsehoods were needed to equate this with the inconstancy of the flesh. He had often overlooked anything expedient in his loves. He had desired and pursued women who charmed him with their lies and enchanted him with their absolute irresponsibility. He had bought their clothes and their tickets, paid their hairdressers and their landlords and, in one case, a facial surgeon. When he bought some diamond earrings he had deliberately judged the sexual mileage he could expect from these jewels. When women had faults he often found them charming. When, while dieting rigorously and continuously talking about their diet, they are found eating a candy bar in a parking lot, one is enchanted. He did not find Jody's faults enchanting. He did not find them.

His radiant and aching need for Jody spread out from his crotch through every part of him, visible and invisible, and he wondered if he could bring off his love for Jody in the street. Would he walk down the street with his arm around Jody's waist, would he kiss Jody at the airport, would he hold Jody's hand in the elevator, and if he refrained from any of this wouldn't he be conforming to the cruel edicts of a blasphemous society? He tried to imagine Jody and himself in the world. He remembered those pensions or European boardinghouses where he and Marcia and their son sometimes spent the summer. Young men, women, and their children—if they were not young they were at least agile—set the tone. One avoided the company of the old and the infirm. Their haunts were well known and word got around. But here and there, in this familial landscape, one saw at the end of the bar or the corner of the dining room two men or two women. They were the queers, a fact that was usually established by some conspicuous dynamism of opposites. One of the women would be docile; the other commanding. One of the men would be old; the other a boy. One was terribly polite to them, but they were never asked to crew in the sailboat races or take a picnic up the mountain. They were not even asked to the marriage of the village blacksmith. They were different. How they gratified their venereal hungers would remain, for the rest of the company, acrobatic and bizarre. They would not, as the rest of the company did, inaugurate the siesta with a good, sweaty fuck. Socially the prejudice against them was very light; at a more profound level it was absolute. That they enjoyed one another's company, as they sometimes did, seemed astonishing and subversive. At one pension Farragut remembered, the queers seemed to be the only happy couple in the dining room. That had been a bad season for holy matrimony. The wives wept. The husbands sulked. The queers won the sailboat race, climbed the highest mountain and were asked to lunch by the reigning prince. That was an exception. Farragut—extending things out to the street—tried to imagine Jody and himself at some such pension. It was five. They were at the end of the bar. Jody was wearing a white duck suit that Farragut had bought him; but that was as far as he could go. There was no way he could wrench, twist, screw or otherwise force his imagination to continue the scene.

If love was a chain of resemblances, there was,

since Jody was a man, the danger that Farragut might be in love with himself. He had seen self-love only once that he could remember in a man, someone he had worked with for a year or so. The man played a role of no consequence in his affairs and he had, perhaps to his disadvantage, only casually observed this fault, if it was a fault. "Have you ever noticed," the man had asked, "that one of my eyes is smaller than the other?" Later the man had asked with some intensity: "Do you think I'd look better with a beard, a mustache perhaps?" Walking down a sidewalk to a restaurant, the man had asked: "Do you like your shadow? When the sun is behind me and I see my shadow I'm always disappointed. My shoulders aren't broad enough and my hips are too wide." Swimming together, the man asked: "Frankly now, what do you think of my biceps? I mean do you think they're overdeveloped? I do forty push-ups every morning to keep them firm, but I wouldn't want to look like a weight lifter." These questions were not continuous, they were not even daily, but they came often enough to appear eccentric and had led Farragut to wonder, and then to the conviction that the man was in love with himself. He spoke about himself as some other man, in a chancy marriage, might ask for approval of his wife. Do you think she's beautiful? Do you think she talks too much? Don't you like her legs? Do you think she ought to cut her hair? Farragut did not think that he was in love with himself, but once, when he got off the mattress to piss, Jody had said, "Shit, man, you're beautiful. I mean you're practically senile and there isn't much light in here, but you look very beautiful to me." Bullshit, said Farragut, but in some part of the considerable wilderness that was himself, a flower seemed to bloom and he could not find the blossom and crush it with his heel. It was a whore's line, he knew, but he seemed helplessly susceptible. It seemed that he had always known he was beautiful and had been waiting all his life to hear this said. But if in loving Jody he loved himself, there was that chance that he might, hell for leather, have become infatuated with his lost youth. Jody posed as a youth, he had the sweet breath and the sweet-smelling skin of youth, and in possessing these Farragut possessed an hour of greenness. He missed his youth, missed it as he would miss a friend, a lover, a rented house on one of the great beaches where he had been a young man. To embrace one's self, one's youth, might be easier than to love a fair woman whose nature was rooted in a past that he could never comprehend. In loving Mildred, for example, he had had to learn to accommodate her taste for anchovies at breakfast, scalding bath water, tardy orgasms, and lemon-yellow wallpaper, toilet paper, bed linen, lampshades, dinner plates, table linen, upholstery and cars. She had even bought him a lemon-yellow jockstrap. To love oneself would be an idle, an impossible, but a delicious pursuit. How simple to love oneself!

And then there was to think upon the courting of death and death's dark simples, that in covering Jody's body he willingly embraced decay and corruption. To kiss a man on the throat, to gaze into a man's eyes with passion, was as unnatural as the rites and procedures in a funeral parlor; while kissing, as he had, the tight skin of Jody's belly, he might have been kissing the turf that would cover him.

With Jody gone—with the removal of this erotic and sentimental schedule—Farragut found his sense of time and space somewhat imperiled. He owned a watch and a calendar and his surroundings had never been so easily catalogued, but he had never faced with such deep apprehension the fact that he did not know where he was. He was at the head of a slalom trail, he was waiting for a train, he was waking after a bad drug trip in a hotel in New Mexico. "Hey, Tiny," he would shout, "where am I?" Tiny understood. "Falconer Prison," he would say. "You killed your brother." "Thanks, Tiny." So, on the strength of Tiny's voice, the bare facts would return. In order to lessen this troubling sense of otherness, he remembered that he had experienced this in the street as well. The sense of being simultaneously in two or three places at the same instant was something he had known beyond the walls. He remembered standing in an air-conditioned office on a sunny day while he seemed, at the same time, to be standing in a shabby farmhouse at the beginning of a blizzard. He could, standing in a highly disinfected office, catch the smell of a woodbox and catalogue his legitimate concerns about tire chains, snowplows and supplies of groceries, fuel and liquor—everything that concerns a man in a remote house at the beginning of a tempest. This was a memory, of course, seizing someplace in the present, but why should he, in an antiseptic room in midsummer, have unwillingly received such a memory? He tried to track it down on the evidence of smell.

A wooden match burning in an ashtray might have provoked the memory, and he had been skeptical about his sensual responsiveness ever since he had, while watching the approach of a thunderstorm, been disconcerted by a wet and implacable erection. But if he could explain this duality by the smoke of a burning match, he could not explain that the vividness of his farmhouse memory deeply challenged the reality of the office where he stood. To weaken and dispel the unwanted memory, he forced his mind beyond the office, which was indeed artificial, to the incontestable fact that it was the nineteenth of July, the temperature outside was ninety-two, the time was three-eighteen and he had eaten for lunch scallops or cod cheeks with sweet tartar sauce, sour fried potatoes, salad, half a roll with butter, ice cream and coffee. Armed with these indisputable details, he seemed to scourge the farmhouse memory as one opens doors and windows to get the smoke out of a room. He was successful at establishing the reality of the office and while he was not truly uneasy about the experience, it had very definitely raised a question for which he had no information at all.

With the exception of organized religion and triumphant fucking, Farragut considered transcendent experience to be perilous rubbish. One saved one's ardor for people and objects that could be used. The flora and fauna of the rain forest were incomprehensible, but one could comprehend the path that led to one's destination. However, at Falconer the walls and the bars had sometimes seemed to threaten to vanish, leaving him with a nothingness that would be worse. He was, for example, waked early one morning by the noise of the toilet and found himself among the receding fragments of some dream. He was not sure of the depth of the dream—of its profundity—but he had never (nor had his psychiatrists) been able to clearly define the moraines of consciousness that compose the shores of waking. In the dream he saw the face of a beautiful woman he enjoyed but had never much loved. He also saw or felt the presence of one of the great beaches on a sea island. A nursery rhyme or jingle was being sung. He pursued these receding fragments as if his life, his self-esteem, depended upon his bringing them together into a coherent and useful memory. They fled, they fled purposefully like the carrier in a football game, and one by one he saw the woman and the presence of the sea disappear and heard the music of the jingle fade away. He checked his watch. It was three-ten. The commotion in the toilet subsided. He fell asleep.

Days, weeks, months or whatever later, he waked from the same dream of the woman, the beach and the song, pursued them with the same intensity that he had in the beginning, and one by one lost them while the music faded. Imperfectly remembered dreams—if they were pursued—were a commonplace, but the dispersal of this dream was unusually deep and vivid. He asked himself, from his psychiatric experience, if the dream was in color. It had been, but not brilliantly. The sea had been dark and the woman wore no lipstick, but the memory was not limited to black and white. He missed the dream. He was genuinely irritated at the fact that he had lost it. It was, of course, worthless, but it seemed like a talisman. He checked his watch and saw that it was three-ten. The toilet was still. He went back to sleep.

This happened again and again and perhaps again. The time was not always precisely three-ten, but it was always between three and four in the morning. He was always left irritable at the fact that his memory could, quite independently of anything he knew about himself, manipulate its resources in controlled and repeated designs. His memory enjoyed free will, and his irritability was increased by his realization that his memory was as unruly as his genitals. Then one morning, jogging from the mess to shop along the dark tunnel, he heard the music and saw the woman and the sea. He stopped so abruptly that several men banged into him, scattering the dream galley-west. That was that for the morning. But the dream was to reappear again and again in different places around the prison. Then one evening in his cell, as he was reading Descartes, he heard the music and waited for the woman and the sea. The cellblock was quiet. The circumstances for concentration were perfect. He reasoned that if he could pin down a line or two of the jingle, he would be able to reassemble the rest of the reverie. The words and the music were receding, but he was able to keep abreast of their retreat. He grabbed a pencil and a scrap of paper and was about to write down the lines he had captured when he realized that he did not know who or where he was, that the uses of the toilet he faced were completely mysterious, and that he could not understand a word of the book he held in his hands. He did not know himself. He did not know his own language. He abruptly stopped his pursuit of the woman and the music and was relieved to have them disappear. They took with them the absolute experience of alienation, leaving him with a light nausea. He was more shaken than wounded. He picked up the book and found that he could read. The toilet was for waste. The prison was called Falconer. He was convicted of murder. One by one he gathered up the details of the moment. They were not particularly sweet, but they were useful and durable. He did not know what would have happened had he copied down the words of the song. Neither death nor madness seemed involved, but he did not feel committed to discover what would happen if he pieced the reverie together. The reverie returned to him again and again, but he shrugged it off vigorously since it had nothing to do with the path he took or his destination.

"Knock, knock," said the Cuckold. It was late, but Tiny hadn't called lockup. Chicken Number Two and the Mad Dog Killer were playing rummy. Television was shit. The Cuckold came into Farragut's cell and sat in the chair. Farragut disliked him. His round pink face and his thin hair had not been changed at all by prison. The brilliant pinkness of the Cuckold, his protuberant vulnerability—produced, it seemed, by alcohol and sexual embarrassment—had not lost its striking hue. "You miss Jody?" he asked. Farragut said nothing. "You score with Jody?" Farragut said nothing. "Hell, man, I know you do," said the Cuckold, "but I don't hold it against you. He was beautiful, he was just beautiful. Do you mind if I talk?"

"I've got a cab downstairs, waiting to take me to the airport," said Farragut. Then he said, sincerely, "No, no, no, I don't mind if you talk, I don't mind at all."

"I scored with a man," said the Cuckold. "That was after I had left my wife. That time I found her screwing this kid on the floor of the front hall. My thing with this man began in a Chinese restaurant. In those days I was the kind of lonely man you see eating in Chinese restaurants. You know? Anywhere in this country and in some parts of Europe where I've been. The Chung Fu Dynasty. The One Hung Low. Paper lanterns with teakwood frames all over the place. Sometimes they keep the Christmas lights up all year round. Paper flowers, many paper flowers. Large family groups. Also oddballs. Fat women. Square pegs. Jews. Sometimes lovers and always this lonely man. Me. We never eat the Chinese food, we lonely men. We always have the London broil or the Boston baked beans in Chinese restaurants. We're international. Anyhow, I'm a lonely man eating the London broil in a Chinese restaurant on the strip outside Kansas City. Any place that used to have a local option has a place outside the town limits where you used to have to go for liquor, cunt, a motel bed for a couple of hours.

"The place, this Chinese restaurant, is about half full. At a table is this young man. That's about it. He's good-looking, but that's because he's young. He'll look like the rest of the world in ten years. But he keeps looking at me and smiling. I honestly don't know what he's after. So then when I get my pineapple chunks, each one with a toothpick, and my fortune cookie, he comes over to my table and asks me what my fortune is. So I tell him I can't read my fortune without my glasses and I don't have my glasses and so he takes this scrap of paper and he reads or pretends to read that my fortune is I am going to have a beautiful adventure within the next hour. So I ask him what his fortune is and he says it's the same thing. He goes on smiling. He speaks real nicely but you could tell he was poor. You could tell that speaking nicely was something he learned. So when I go out he goes out with me. He asks where I'm staying at and I say I'm staying at this motel which is attached to the restaurant. Then he asks if I have anything to drink in my room and I say yes, would he like a drink, and he says he'd love a drink and he puts his arm around my shoulder, very buddy-buddy, and we go to my room. So then he says can he make the drinks and I say sure and I tell him where the whiskey and the ice is and he makes some nice drinks and sits beside me and begins to kiss me on the face. Now, the idea of men kissing one another doesn't go down with me at all, although it gave me no pain. I mean a man kissing a woman is a plus and minus situation, but a man kissing a man except maybe in France is a very worthless two of a kind. I mean if someone took a picture of this fellow kissing me it would be for me a very strange and unnatural picture, but why should my cock have begun to put on weight if it was all so strange and unnatural? So then I thought what could be more strange and unnatural than a man eating baked beans alone in a Chinese restaurant in the Middle West—this was something I didn't invent—and when he felt for my cock, nicely and gently, and went on kissing me, my cock put on its maximum weight and began pouring out juice and when I felt of him he was halfway there.

"So then he made some more drinks and asked me why I didn't take off my clothes and I said what about him and he dropped his pants displaying a very beautiful cock and I took off my clothes and we sat bare-ass on the sofa drinking our drinks. He made a lot of drinks. Now and then he would take my cock in his mouth and this was the first time in my life that I ever had a mouth around my cock. I thought this would look like hell in a newsreel or on the front page of the newspaper, but evidently my cock hadn't ever seen a newspaper because it was going crazy. So then he suggested that we get into bed and we did and the next thing I knew the telephone was ringing and it was morning.

"It was all dark. I was alone. I had a terrible headache. I picked up the telephone and a voice said, 'The time is now seven-thirty.' Then I felt around in bed to see if there was any evidence of a come but there wasn't. Then I went to the closet and looked at my wallet and all the money—about fifty dollars—was gone. Nothing else, none of my credit cards. So the hustler had teased me, given me a Mickey Finn and taken off with my money. I lost fifty dollars but I guessed I'd learned something. So while I was shaving the phone rang. It was the hustler. You'd think I'd be angry with him, wouldn't you, but I was all sweetness and friendliness. First he said he was sorry that he made my drinks so strong I had passed out. Then he said I shouldn't have given him all that money, that he wasn't worth it. Then he said he was sorry, that he wanted to give me a marvelous time for free, and when could we meet. So I knew he had teased me and stoned me and robbed me, but I wanted him badly and I said I would be in at about half-past five and why didn't he come around then.

"I had four calls to make that day and I made them and I made three sales, which was good for that territory. I was feeling all right when I got back to the motel and I had some drinks and he came in at half-past five and I mixed his drinks this time. He laughed when I did this but I didn't say anything about the Mickey. Then he took off his clothes and folded them neatly on a chair and he took off my clothes with some assistance from me and kissed me all over. Then he got a look at himself in the big mirror on the bathroom door and this was the first time I ever saw a man who was narcissistic, what they call. One look at himself naked in the mirror and he couldn't get away. He couldn't get enough of it. He couldn't tear himself away. So then I figured out my options. I had cashed a check and I had about sixty dollars in my wallet. I had to hide this. While he was loving himself I was worried about money. Then when I saw how deep he was, how really absorbed he was in the way he looked, I picked my clothes up off the floor and hung them in the closet. He didn't notice me, he didn't see anything but himself. So there he was, fondling his balls in the mirror, and there I was in the closet. I took the cash out of my wallet and stuffed it into the toe of my shoe. So then he finally separated from himself in the looking glass and joined me on the sofa and loved me up and when I came I nearly blew my eyeballs out. So then we got dressed and went out to the Chinese restaurant.

"When I got dressed I had some trouble getting into my shoe with the sixty dollars in the toe. I had credit cards to pay for dinner. When we walked to the restaurant he said why are you limping and I said I wasn't limping, but I guessed he knew where the money was. They took Carte Blanche at the restaurant and so I wasn't a lonely man in a Chinese restaurant anymore, I was an old queer with a young queer in a Chinese restaurant. I've been looking down my nose at couples like this all my life, but I've felt worse. We had this very big, very good dinner and so then I paid the check with my Carte Blanche and he said didn't I have any cash and I said no, I'd given it all to him, hadn't I, and he laughed and we went back to my room although I was very careful not to limp and wondered what I would do with the sixty dollars because I wasn't going to pay him that much. So then I hid my shoe in a dark corner and we got into bed and he loved me up again and then we talked and I asked him who he was and he told me.

"He said his name was Giuseppe or Joe but he changed it to Michael. His father was Italian. His mother was white. His father had a dairy farm in Maine. He went to school but he worked for his father in his time off and he was about nine when the chief at the dairy farm started to blow him. He liked it and it got to be a daily thing until the dairy chief asked him if he would take it up the ass. He was eleven or twelve then. It took four or five tries before he got it all the

way in but when it worked it felt wonderful and they
did this all the time. But it was a very hard life going to
school and working on the farm and never seeing anybody but the dairy chief so then he began to hustle, first
in the nearest town and then the nearest city and then
all the way across the country and around the world.
He said that that's what he was, a hustler, and that I
shouldn't feel sorry for him or wonder what would
become of him.

"All the time he was talking I listened very carefully to him, expecting him to sound like a fairy, but he
never did, not that I could hear. I have this very strong
prejudice against fairies. I've always thought they were
silly and feeble-minded, but he talked like anybody else.
I was really very interested in what he had to say
because he seemed to me very gentle and affectionate
and even very pure. Lying in bed with me that night he
seemed to me about the purest person I have ever
known because he didn't have any conscience at all, I
guess I mean he didn't have any prefabricated conscience. He just moved through it all like a swimmer
through pure water. So then he said he was sleepy and
tired and I said I was sleepy and tired and he said he
was sorry he robbed me of the money but he hoped he'd
made it up to me and I said he had and then he said
that he knew I had some cash in my shoe but that he
wasn't going to steal it and that I shouldn't worry and
so we fell asleep. It was a nice sleep and when we woke
in the morning I made some coffee and we joked and
shaved and dressed and there was all the money in my
shoe and I said I was late and he said he was late too
and I said late for what and he said he had a client wait-

ing in room 273 and then he asked did I mind and I
said no, I guessed I didn't mind, and then he said could
we meet at around half-past five and I said sure.

"So he went his way and I went mine and I made
five sales that day and I thought that he wasn't only
pure, he was lucky, and I felt very happy coming back
to the motel and I took a shower and had a couple of
drinks. There was no sign of him at half-past five and
no sign of him at half-past six or seven and I guessed
he'd found a customer who didn't keep his money in his
shoe and I missed him, but then sometime after seven
the phone rang and I slid a base to get it, thinking it
was Michael, but it was the police. They asked if I
knew him and I said sure I knew him, because I did. So
then they asked could I come down to the county courthouse and I asked what for and they said they'd tell me
when I got there so I said I would be there. I asked the
man in the lobby how to get to the county courthouse
and he told me and then I drove there. I thought perhaps he'd been picked up on some charge like vagrancy
and needed bail and I was willing, I was willing and
eager to bail him out. So when I spoke to the lieutenant
who called me he was nice enough but also sad and he
said how well did I know Michael and I said I'd met
him at the Chinese restaurant and had some drinks
with him. He said they weren't charging me with anything but did I know him well enough to identify him
and I said of course, thinking that he might be in some
line-up although I had already begun to sense that it
would be something more serious and grave, as it was.
I followed him down some stairs and I could tell by the
stink where we were going and there were all these big

drawers like a walk-in filing cabinet and he pulled one out and there was Michael, very dead, of course. The lieutenant said they got him with a knife in the back, twenty-two times, and the cop, the lieutenant, said he was very big in drugs, very active, and I guess somebody really hated him. They must have gone on knifing him long after he was dead. So then the lieutenant and I shook hands and I think he gave me a searching look to see if I was an addict or a queer and then he gave me a broad smile of relief which meant that he didn't think I was either although I could have made this all up. I went back to the motel and had about seventeen more drinks and cried myself to sleep."

It was not that night but sometime later that the Cuckold told Farragut about the Valley. The Valley was a long room off the tunnel to the left of the mess hall. Along one wall was a cast-iron trough of a urinal. The light in the room was very dim. The wall above the urinal was white tiling with a very limited power of reflection. You could make out the height and the complexion of the men on your left and your right and that was about all. The Valley was where you went after chow to fuck yourself. Almost no one but killjoys strayed into the dungeon for a simple piss. There were ground rules. You could touch the other man's hips and shoulders, but nothing else. The trough accommodated twenty men and twenty men stood there, soft, hard or halfway in either direction, fucking themselves. If you finished and wanted to come again you went to the end of the line. There were the usual jokes. How many times, Charlie? Five coming up, but my feet are getting sore.

Considering the fact that the cock is the most critical link in our chain of survival, the variety of shapes, colors, sizes, characteristics, dispositions and responses found in this rudimentary tool are much greater than those shown by any other organ of the body. They were black, white, red, yellow, lavender, brown, warty, wrinkled, comely and silken, and they seemed, like any crowd of men on a street at closing time, to represent youth, age, victory, disaster, laughter and tears. There were the frenzied and compulsive pumpers, the long-timers who caressed themselves for half an hour, there were the groaners and the ones who sighed, and most of the men, when their trigger was pulled and the fusillade began, would shake, buck, catch their breath and make weeping sounds, sounds of grief, of joy, and sometimes death rattles. There was some rightness in having the images of the lovers around them opaque. They were universal, they were phantoms, and any skin sores, or signs of cruelty, ugliness, stupidity or beauty, could not be seen. Farragut went here regularly after Jody was gone.

When Farragut arced or pumped his rocks into the trough he endured no true sadness—mostly some slight disenchantment at having spilled his energy onto iron. Walking away from the trough, he felt that he had missed the train, the plane, the boat. He had missed it. He experienced some marked physical relief or improvement: the shots cleared his brain. Shame and remorse had nothing to do with what he felt, walking away from the trough. What he felt, what he saw, was the utter poverty of erotic reasonableness. That was how he missed the target and the target was the mysteriousness of the bonded spirit and the flesh. He knew it well. Fitness and beauty had a rim. Fitness and beauty had a dimension, had a floor, even as the oceans have a floor, and he had committed a trespass. It was not unforgivable—a venal trespass—but he was reproached by the majesty of the realm. It was majestic; even in prison he knew the world to be majestic. He had taken a pebble out of his shoe in the middle of mass. He remembered the panic he had experienced as a boy when he found his trousers, his hands and his shirttails soaked with crystallizing gism. He had learned from the *Boy Scout Handbook* that his prick would grow as long and thin as a shoelace, and that the juice that had poured out of his crack was the cream of his brain power. This miserable wetness proved that he would fail his College Board exams and have to attend a broken-down agricultural college somewhere in the Middle West. . . .

Then Marcia returned in her limitless beauty, smelling of everything provocative. She did not kiss him, nor did he try to cover her hand with his. "Hello, Zeke," she said. "I have a letter here from Pete."

"How is he?"

"He seems very well. He's either away at school or camp and I don't see anything of him. His advisers tell me that he is friendly and intelligent."

"Can he come to see me?"

"They think not, not at this time of his life. Every

psychiatrist and counselor I've talked with, and I've been very conscientious about this, feels that since he's an only child, the experience of visiting his father in prison would be crippling. I know you have no use for psychologists, and I'm inclined to agree with you, but all we can do is to take the advice of the most highly recommended and experienced men, and that is their opinion."

"Can I see his letter?"

"You can if I can find it. I haven't been able to find anything today. I don't believe in poltergeists, but there are days when I can find things and there are days when I cannot. Today is one of the worst. I couldn't find the top to the coffeepot this morning. I couldn't find the oranges. Then I couldn't find the car keys and when I found them and drove to get the cleaning woman I couldn't remember where she lived. I couldn't find the dress I wanted, I couldn't find my earrings. I couldn't find my stockings and I couldn't find my glasses to look for my stockings." He might have killed her then had she not found an envelope on which his name was written clumsily in lead pencil. She put this on the counter. "I didn't ask him to write the letter," she said, "and I have no idea of what it contains. I suppose I should have shown it to the counselors, but I knew you would rather I didn't."

"Thank you," said Farragut. He put the letter into his shirt, next to his skin.

"Aren't you going to open it?"

"I'll save it."

"Well, you're lucky. So far as I know, it's the first letter he's ever written in his life. So tell me how you

are, Zeke. I can't say that you look well, but you look all
right. You look very much like yourself. Do you still
dream about your blonde? You do, of course; that I can
easily see. Don't you understand that she never existed,
Zeke, and that she never will? Oh, I can tell by the way
you hold your head that you still dream about that
blonde who never menstruated or shaved her legs or
challenged anything you said or did. I suppose you
have boyfriends in here?"

"I've had one," said Farragut, "but I didn't take it up
the ass. When I die you can put on my headstone:
'Here lies Ezekiel Farragut, who never took it up the
ass.'"

She seemed suddenly touched by this, suddenly she
seemed to find in herself some admiration for him; her
smile and her presence seemed accommodating and
soft. "Your hair has turned white, dear," she said. "Did
you know that? You haven't been here a year and yet
your hair has turned snow white. It's very becoming.
Well, I'll have to go. I've left your groceries in the
package room." He carried the letter until the lights
and the television were extinguished and read, in the
glare from the yard, "I love you."

As the day of the cardinal's arrival approached,
even the lifers said they had never seen such excitement. Farragut was kept busy cutting dittos for order
sheets, instructions and commands. Some of the orders
seemed insane. For example: "It is mandatory that all
units of inmates marching to and from the parade
grounds will sing God Bless America." Common sense
killed this one. No one obeyed the order and no one
tried to enforce it. Every day for ten days the entire

population was marshaled out onto the gallows field, the ball park, and what had now become the parade grounds. They were made to practice standing at attention, even in the pouring rain. They remained excited, and there was a large element of seriousness in the excitement. When Chicken Number Two did a little hornpipe and sang: "Tomorrow's the day they give cardinals away with a half a pound of cheese," no one laughed, no one at all. Chicken Number Two was an asshole. On the day before his arrival, every man took a shower. The hot water ran out at around eleven in the morning and cellblock F didn't get into the showers until after chow. Farragut was back in his cell, shining his shoes, when Jody returned.

He heard the hooting and whistling and looked up to see Jody walking toward his cell. Jody had put on weight. He looked well. He walked toward Farragut with his nice, bouncy jock walk. Farragut much preferred this to the sinuous hustle Jody put on when he was hot and his pelvis seemed to grin like a pumpkin. The sinuous hustle had reminded Farragut of vines, and vines, he knew, had to be cultivated or they could harass and destroy stone towers, castles and cathedrals. Vines could pull down a basilica. Jody came into his cell and kissed him on the mouth. Only Chicken Number Two whistled. "Goodbye, sweetheart," he said. "Goodbye," said Farragut. His feelings were chaotic and he might have cried, but he might have cried at the death of a cat, a broken shoelace, a wild pitch. He could kiss Jody passionately, but not tenderly. Jody turned and walked away. Farragut had done nothing with Jody so exciting as to say goodbye. Among the beaches and graves and other matters he had unearthed in seeking the meaning of his friendship, he had completely overlooked the conspiratorial thrill of seeing his beloved escape.

Tiny called the lockup for eight and made the usual jokes about beauty sleep and meat-beating. He said, of course, that he wanted his men to look beautiful for the cardinal. He pulled the light switch at nine. The only light was the television. Farragut went to bed and to sleep. The roar of the toilet woke him and then he heard thunder. At first the noise pleased and excited him. The random explosions of thunder seemed to explain that heaven was not an infinity but a solid construction of domes, rotundas and arches. Then he remembered that the flier had said that in case of rain the ceremony would be canceled. The thought of a thunderstorm inaugurating a rainy day deeply disturbed him. Naked, he went to the window. This naked man was worried. If it rained there would be no escape, no cardinal, no nothing. Have pity upon him, then; try to understand his fears. He was lonely. His love, his world, his everything, was gone. He wanted to see a cardinal in a helicopter. Thunderstorms, he thought hopefully, could bring in anything. They could bring in a cold front, a hot front, a day when the clearness of the light would seem to carry one from hour to hour. Then the rain began. It poured into the prison and that part of the world. But it lasted only ten minutes. Then the rain, the storm, swept mercifully off to the north and just as swiftly and just as briefly that rank and vigorous odor that is detonated by the rain flew up to and above where Farragut stood at his barred window.

He had, with his long, long nose, responded to this
cutting fragrance wherever he had been—shouting,
throwing out his arms, pouring a drink. Now there was
a trace, a memory, of this primitive excitement, but it
had been cruelly eclipsed by the bars. He got back into
bed and fell asleep, listening to the rain dripping from
the gun towers.

Farragut got what he had bargained for: a day of
incomparable beauty. Had he been a free man, he
would have claimed to be able to walk on the light. It
was a holiday; it was the day of the big Rugby game; it
was the circus; it was the fourth of July; it was the
regatta; and it dawned as it should, clear and cool and
beautiful. They had two pieces of bacon for breakfast,
through the bounty of the diocese. Farragut went down
the tunnel to the methadone line and even this rat tail
of humanity seemed to be jumping with high spirits. At
eight they stood by their cell doors, shaved, wearing
their white shirts and some of them with ointment in
their hair, you could tell by the clash of perfumes that
floated up and down the cellblock. Tiny inspected them
and then there was, as there is for any holiday or
ceremony, time to kill.

There was a cartoon show on television. They could
hear whistles blowing on other cellblocks and guards
with military backgrounds trying to shout their men
into sharp formations. It was only a little after eight
then and the cardinal wasn't expected until noon, but
men were already being marched out onto the gallows
field. The walls checked the force of the late spring

sun, but it would hit the field by noon. Chicken and the Cuckold shot dice. Farragut killed the time easily at the top of his methadone high. Time was new bread, time was a sympathetic element, time was water you swam in, time moved through the cellblock with the grace of light. Farragut tried to read. He sat on the edge of his bunk. He was a man of forty-eight, sitting on the edge of his bunk in a prison to which he had been unjustly confined for the murder of his brother. He was a man in a white shirt sitting on the edge of a bunk. Tiny blew his whistle and they stood at attention in front of their cells again. They did this four times. At half-past ten they were lined up two by two and marched down the tunnel, where they formed up in a pie-shaped area marked "F" with lime.

The light had begun to come into the field. Oh, it was a great day. Farragut thought about Jody and wondered if he didn't bring it off would he get cell lock or the hole or maybe seven more years for attempted escape. So far as he knew, he and the chaplain's dude were the only ones in on the plot. Then Tiny called them to attention. "Now, I got to have your coopera- tion," Tiny said. "It ain't easy for any of us to have two thousand shit-heads out here together. The tower guards today is been replaced with crack shots and, as you know, they got the right to shoot any inmate they got suspicions about. We got crack shots today so they won't be no spray firing. The leader of the Black Panthers has agreed not to give the salute. When the cardinal comes you stand at parade rest. Any of you ain't been in the service, ask some friend what parade rest is. It's like this. Twenty-five men has been picked to take the Holy Eucharist. The cardinal's got lots of appointments and he's going to be here only twenty minutes. First we hear from the warden and then the commissioner, who's coming down from Albany. After this he gives out the diplomas, celebrates mass, blesses the rest of you assholes and takes off. I guess you can sit down if you want. You can sit down, but when you get the order for attention I want you all straight and neat and clean with your heads up. I want to be proud of you. If you have to piss, piss, but don't piss where anybody's going to be sitting." Cheers for Tiny and then most of them pissed. There was, Farragut thought, some universality to a full bladder. For this length of time they perfectly understood one another. Then they sat down.

Somebody was testing the public address system: "Testing, one, two, three. Testing, one, two, three." The voice was loud and scratchy. Time passed. God's advocate was punctual. At a quarter to twelve they got the command for attention. They shaped up nicely. The sound of the chopper could be heard then, bounding off the hills, loud at low altitudes, faintly, faintly in the deep river valley; soft and loud, hills and valleys, the noise evoked the contour of the terrain beyond the walls. The chopper, when it came into view, had no more grace than an airborne washing machine, but this didn't matter at all. It lofted gently onto the target and out the door came three acolytes, a monsignor in black, and the cardinal himself, a man either graced by God with great dignity and beauty or singled out by the diocese for these distinctions. He raised his hand. His ring flashed with spiritual and political power. "I seen better rings on hustlers," Chicken Number Two whispered. "No fence would give you thirty. The last time I hit a jewelry store I fenced the lot for—" Looks shut him up. Everybody turned and put him down.

The crimson of the cardinal's robes seemed living and pure and his carriage was admirable and would have quelled a riot. He stepped out of the helicopter, lifting his robes not at all like a woman leaving a taxi but like a cardinal leaving his airborne transport. He made a sign of the cross as high and wide as his reach and the great spell of worship fell over that place. *In nomine Patris et Filii et Spiritus Sancti.* Farragut would have liked to pray for the happiness of his son, his wife, the safety of his lover, the soul of his dead brother, would have liked to pray for some enlargement of his wisdom, but the only word he could root out of these massive intentions was his *Amen. Amen,* said a thousand others, and the word, from so many throats, came up from the gallows field as a solemn whisper.

Then the public address system began to work so well that the confusion that followed could be heard by everyone. "Now you go first," said the commissioner to the warden. "No, you go," said the warden to the commissioner. "It says here that you go." "I said you go," said the commissioner angrily to the warden, and the warden stepped forward, knelt, kissed the cardinal's ring and, standing, said: "The graciousness of Your Eminence in endangering life and limb in order to come and visit us in the Falconer Rehabilitation Center is greatly appreciated by me and the deputy wardens, the guards and all the inmates. It reminds me of how when I was a little boy and sleepy my father carried me from the car into the house at the end of a long trip. I was a load to carry, but I knew how kind he was being to me, and that's the way I feel today."

There was applause—exactly the noise of water striking stone—but unlike the indecipherable noise of water, its intent was clearly grateful and polite. Farragut remembered applause most vividly when he had heard it outside the theater, hall or church where it sounded. He had heard it most clearly as a bystander waiting in a parking lot on a summer night, waiting for the show to break. It had always astonished and deeply moved him to realize that so diverse and warlike a people could have agreed on this signal of enthusiasm and assent. The warden passed the public address system to the commissioner. The commissioner had gray hair, wore a gray suit and a gray tie, and reminded Farragut of the grayness and angularity of office filing cabinets in the far, far away. "Your Eminence," he said, reading his speech from a paper and evidently for the first time. "Ladies and gentlemen." He frowned, raised his face and his heavy eyebrows at this error of his speech writer. "Gentlemen!" he exclaimed. "I want to express my gratitude and the gratitude of the governor to the cardinal, who for the first time in the history of this diocese and perhaps in the whole history of mankind has visited a rehabilitation center in a helicopter. The governor sends his sincere regrets at not being able to express his gratitude in person, but he is, as you must all know, touring the flood-disaster areas in the northwestern part of the state. We hear these days"— he picked up a head of steam—"a great deal about prison reform. Best sellers are written about prison reform. Professional so-called penologists travel from coast to coast, speaking on prison reform. But where does prison reform begin? In bookstores? In lecture halls? *No.* Prison reform, like all sincere endeavors at reform, begins at home, and where is home? Home is prison! We have come here today to commemorate a bold step made possible by the Fiduciary University of Banking, the archdiocese, the Department of Correction and above all the prisoners themselves. All four of us together have accomplished what we might compare—compare only, of course—to a miracle. These eight humble men have passed with honors a most difficult test that many well-known captains of industry have failed. Now, I know that you all have, unwillingly, sacrificed your right to vote upon coming here—a sacrifice that the governor intends to change—and should you, at some later date, find his name on a ballot I'm sure you will remember today." He shot his cuff to check the time. "As I present these coveted diplomas, please refrain from applause until the presentation is completed. Frank Masullo, Herman Meany, Mike Thomas, Henry Phillips . . ." When the last of the diplomas had been presented, he lowered his voice in a truly moving shift from secular to spiritual matters and said, "His Eminence will now celebrate mass." At exactly that moment Jody came out of the boiler room behind the bench, genuflected deeply at the cardinal's back and took his place at the right of the altar, the consummate figure of a tardy acolyte who has just taken a piss.

Adiutorium nostrum in Nomine Domini. The raptness of prayer enthralled Farragut as the raptness of love. *Misereatur tui omnipotens Deus et dismissis pecatis tuis. Misereatur vestri omnipotens Deus et dismissis pecatis vestris perducat vos ad vitam aeternam. Indulgentiam, absolutionem, et remissionem pecatorum nostrorum tribuat nobis omnipotens et misericors Dominus. Deus tu conversus vivificabis nos. Ostende nobis, Domine misericordiam tuam.* On it drummed to the *Benedicat* and the last *Amen.* Then he performed another large cross and returned to the helicopter, followed by his retinue, including Jody.

The props kicked up a cloud of dust and the engine ascended. Someone put a recording of cathedral bells on the public address system and up they went to this glorious clamor. Oh, glory, glory, glory! The exaltation of the bells conquered the scratching of the needle and a slight warp in the record. The sound of the chopper and the bells filled heaven and earth. They all cheered and cheered and cheered and some of them cried. The sound of the bells stopped, but the chopper went on playing its geodetic survey of the surrounding terrain— the shining, lost and beloved world.

The cardinal's helicopter landed at La Guardia, where two large cars were waiting. Jody had seen cars like this in the movies and nowhere else. His Eminence and the monsignor took one. The acolytes filled the second. Jody's excitement was violent. He was shaking. He tried to narrow his thinking down to two points. He would get drunk. He would get laid. He held to these two points with some success, but his palms were sweaty, his ribs were running with sweat and sweat ran down his brows into his eyes. He held his hands together to conceal their shaking. He was afraid that when the car reached its destination he would be unable to walk as a free man. He had forgotten how. He imagined that the paving would fly up and strike him between the eyes. He then convinced himself that he was playing a part in a miracle, that there was some congruence between his escape and the will of God. Play it by ear. "Where are we going?" he asked one of the others. "To the cathedral, I guess," he said. "That's where we left our clothes. Where did you come from?" "Saint Anselm's," said Jody. "I mean how did you get to the prison?" "I went out early," Jody said. "I went out on the train."

The city out of the car windows looked much wilder and stranger than beautiful. He imagined the length of time it would take—he saw time as a length of road, something measured by surveyors' instruments—before he could move unself-consciously. When the car stopped he opened the door. The cardinal was going up the steps of the cathedral and two of the people on the sidewalk knelt. Jody stepped out of the car. There was no strength at all in his legs. Freedom hit him like a gale wind. He fell to his knees and broke the fall with his hands. "Shit, man, you drunk?" the next acolyte asked. "Fortified wine," said Jody. "That wine was fortified." Then his strength returned, all of it, and he got to his feet and followed the others into the cathedral and to a vestry much like any other. He took off his robe and while the other men put on ties and jackets he tried to invest his white shirt, his issue fatigues and his basketball sneakers with respectability. He did this by bracing his shoulders. He saw himself in a long glass and he saw that he looked emphatically like an escaped convict. There was nothing about him—his haircut, his pallor, his dancy step—that a half-blind drunk wouldn't have put down as a prison freak. "His Eminence would like to speak to you," the monsignor said. "Please follow me."

A door was opened and he went into a room a little like the priest's front parlor at home. The cardinal stood there, now in a dark suit, and held out his right hand. Jody knelt and kissed the ring. "Where are you from?" the cardinal asked. "Saint Anselm's, Your Eminence," said Jody. "There is no Saint Anselm's in the diocese," said the cardinal, "but I know where you're from. I don't know why I asked. Time must play an important part in your plans. I expect you have about fifteen minutes. It is exciting, isn't it? Let's get out of here." They left the parlor and the cathedral. On the sidewalk a woman knelt and the cardinal gave her his ring to kiss. She was, Jody saw, an actress he had seen on television. Another woman knelt and kissed his ring before they reached the end of the block. They crossed the street and a third woman knelt and kissed his ring. For her he wearily made a sign of the cross; and then they went into a store. The acknowledgment of their arrival was a matter of seconds. Someone of authority approached them and asked if the cardinal wanted a private room. "I'm not sure," he said. "I'll leave it up to you. This young man and I have an important appointment in fifteen minutes. He is not wearing the right clothes." "We can manage," the authority said. Jody was measured with a tape. "You're built like a tailor's dummy," said the man. This went to Jody's head, but he definitely felt that vanity was out of place in the miracle. Twenty minutes later he walked up Madison Avenue. His walk was springy—the walk of a man going to first on balls, which can, under some circumstances, seem to be a miracle.

It was an August day; a dog day. Rome and Paris would be empty of everyone but tourists, and even the Pope would be taking it easy in Gandolfo. After the methadone line, Farragut went out to cut the big lawn between the education building and cellblock A. He got the mower and the gas tank out of the garage and joked with the Mad Dog Killer. He started the motor with a rope pull, which brought on memories of outboard motors on mountain lakes in the long ago. That was the summer when he had learned to water-ski, not at the stern of an outboard, but at the stern of a racer called a Gar-Wood. He had Christianiaed over the high starboard wake—*bang*—onto a riffled and corrugated stretch of water and then into the dropped curtain of a rain squall. "I have my memories," he said to the lawn mower. "You can't take my memories away from me." One night he and a man named Tony and two girls and a bottle of Scotch raced eight miles down the lake at full throttle—you couldn't have heard thunder—to the excursion boat pier, where there was a big clock face under a sign that said: THE NEXT EXCURSION TO THE NARROWS WILL BE AT . . . They had come to steal the big clock face. It would look great in somebody's bedroom along with the YIELD sign and the DEER CROSSING treasure. Tony was at the helm and Farragut was the appointed thief. He vaulted the gunwale and began to pull at the clock face, but it was securely nailed to the pier. Tony passed Farragut a wrench from the toolbox and he smashed the supports with this, but the noise woke some old watchman, who limped after him while he carried the clock face to the Gar-Wood. "Oh, stop," the old man shouted in his old man's voice. "Stop, stop, stop. Why do you have to do this? Why do you have to destroy everything? Why do you have to make life hard for old men like me? What good is it, what good is it to anybody? What are you doing except to disappoint people and make people angry and cost people money? Stop, stop, stop. Just bring it back and I won't say nothing. Stop, stop. . . ." The noise of the motor, when they escaped, overwhelmed the old man's voice, but Farragut would hear it, more resonant than the Scotch and the girl, for the rest of that night and, he guessed, for the rest of his life. He had described this to the three psychiatrists he had employed. "You see, Dr. Gaspoden, when I heard the old man shouting 'Stop, stop,' I understood my father for the first time in my life. When I heard this old man shouting 'Stop, stop,' I heard my father, I knew how my father felt when I borrowed his tails and went in to lead the cotillion. The voice of this old stranger on a summer night made my father clear to me for the first time in my life." He said all this to the lawn mower.

The day was shit. The air was so heavy that he would put visibility at about two hundred yards. Could it be exploited for an escape? He didn't think so. The thought of escape reminded him of Jody, a remembrance that had remained very light-hearted since he and Jody had passionately kissed goodbye. The administration and perhaps the archdiocese had finessed Jody's departure and he was not even a figure in prison mythology. DiMatteo, the chaplain's dude, had given Farragut the facts. They had met in the tunnel on a dark night when Farragut was leaving the Valley. It was no more than six weeks after Jody's flight. DiMatteo showed him a newspaper photograph of Jody that had been sent to him in the mail. It was Jody on his wedding day—Jody at his most beautiful and triumphant. His stunning brightness shone through the letterpress of some small-town newspaper. His bride was a demure and pretty young Oriental and the caption said that H. Keith Morgan had that day married Sally Chou Lai, the youngest daughter of Ling Chou Lai, president of the Viaduct Wire Factory, where the groom was employed. There was nothing more and Farragut wanted nothing more. He laughed loudly, but not DiMatteo, who said angrily, "He promised to wait for me. I saved his life and he promised to wait for me. He loved me—oh, God, how he loved me. He gave me his golden cross." DiMatteo lifted the cross out of the curls on his chest and showed it to Farragut. Farragut's knowledge of the cross was intimate—it may have borne his tooth marks—and his memories of his lover were vivid, but not at all sad. "He must have married her for her money," said DiMatteo. "She must be rich. He promised to wait for me."

Farragut's mowing of the lawn was planned. Roughly halfway around the circumference of the lawn he reversed his direction so the grass, as it fell, would not heap, dry and discolor. He had heard or read somewhere that cut grass fertilized living grass, although he had observed that dead grass was singularly inert. He walked barefoot because he got better purchase with the soles of his naked feet than he did in prison-issue boots. He had knotted the laces of his boots and hung them around his neck so they wouldn't be stolen and cut into wrist-watch straps. The contrite geometry of grass-cutting pleased him. To cut the grass one followed the contour of the land. To study the contour of the land—to read it as one did on skis—was to study and read the contour of the neighborhood, the county, the state, the continent, the planet, and to study and read the contour of the planet was to study and read the nature of its winds as his old father had done, sailing catboats and kites. Some oneness was involved, some contentment.

When he had finished the big lawn he pushed the mower back to the garage. "They got a riot at The

Wall," said the Killer, stooped above a motor and speaking over his shoulder. "It come over the radio. They got twenty-eight hostages, but it's that time of year. Burn your mattress and get your head broken. It's that time of year."

Farragut jogged up to his cellblock. There was a pleasant stillness there at that hour. Tiny was watching a game show on TV. Farragut stripped off his clothes and washed the sweat off his body with a rag and cold water. "And now," the TV announcer said, "let's take another look at the prizes. First we have the sterling-silver-plated eight-piece Thomas Jefferson coffee service." This was cut into and while Farragut was drawing on his pants, another announcer—a thick-featured young man with yellow hair—said solemnly: "Inmates at the upstate prison of Amana, commonly known as The Wall, have rioted and are holding anywhere from twenty-eight to thirty prison officers as hostages, threatening to cut their throats if their demands are not met. Prison Superintendent John Cooper —I'm sorry—Rehabilitation Facility Superintendent Cooper has agreed to meet the inmates in neutral territory and is awaiting the arrival of Fred D. Emison, head of the State Department of Correction. Stay tuned for further news." The show cut back to a display of more prizes.

Farragut looked at Tiny. His face was white. Farragut cased the cellblock. Tennis, Bumpo and the Stone were in. The Stone was unplugged so that meant that three of them knew. Ransome and Chicken Number Two came in and both of them gave him a look. They knew. Farragut tried to guess what would happen. Any sort of congregation would be forbidden, he guessed, but he guessed that at the same time any provocative disciplines would be side-stepped. Chow would be the first congregation, but when the chow bell rang Tiny opened the cell doors and they headed for the corridor. "Did you hear that on TV?" Tiny asked Farragut. "You mean about the Thomas Jefferson eight-piece sterling-silver-plated coffee service?" asked Farragut. Tiny was sweating. Farragut had gone too far. He was a light-weight. He had blown it. Tiny might have nabbed him then, but he was frightened and Farragut was free to go down to chow. Chow was regulation, but Farragut looked into every face he saw to judge whether or not they knew. He put it at twenty percent. The stir in the mess hall was, he thought, immeasurable, and there were several explosions of hysterical gaiety. One man began to laugh and couldn't stop. He was convulsive. They were given very generous servings of pork in a flour sauce and half a canned pear. "ALL INMATES WILL RETURN TO CELLBLOCK AFTER CHOW FOR FUR-THER ANNOUNCEMENTS. ALL INMATES WILL RETURN TO CELLBLOCK AFTER CHOW FOR FURTHER ANNOUNCE-MENTS." He would have bet on that. Almost everything counted on the next ten minutes, and in the next ten minutes they got them all, so far as Farragut knew, back into their cells. Clang.

Everybody had radios. When they got back to their cells Chicken turned on some loud dance music and stretched out on his cot, smiling. "Kick it, Chicken," Farragut shouted, hoping that if the radio was still no one would notice it. That was dumb because the prob-lem must have been clear to about everyone. Ten min-

utes later they got the announcement. "ALL RADIOS ARE
TO BE TURNED IN TO THE CELLBLOCK OFFICER FOR
TUNE-UP AND FREE REPAIR. ALL RADIOS ARE TO BE
TURNED IN TO THE CELLBLOCK OFFICER FOR TUNE-UP
AND FREE REPAIR." Tiny went down the cellblock and
collected the radios. There were groans and oaths and
the Cuckold tossed his radio through the bars to smash
on the floor. "You feeling good today, Bumpo?" Farragut asked. "You feeling good today, you think today is a
good day?" "No," said Bumpo, "I never liked this humid
weather." He didn't know, then. The phone rang. There
was a message for Farragut. He was to get down to the
office and cut two dittos. Marshack would wait for him
in the squad room.

The tunnel was deserted. Farragut had never seen
it empty. They might all be locked in, but he listened
for the sounds of the inevitable rebellion that would
follow the riot at The Wall. In the distance he thought
he heard shouting and screaming, but when he stopped
and tried to decipher the sound he decided it could be
the sound of traffic outside the walls. There was a faint
siren now and then, but they blew sirens all the time in
the civilian world. As he approached the squad room he
heard a radio. "Inmates have demanded an injunction
against physical and administrative reprisals and a
general amnesty," he heard. Then the radio was cut.
They had either heard him or timed his arrival. Four
officers were sitting around a radio in the squad room.
There were two quarts of whiskey on the desk. The
looks they gave him were blank and hateful. Marshack
—he had small eyes and a shaven skull—gave him two
pieces of paper. Farragut went down the hall to his

office and slammed shut the glass-and-chicken-wire door. As soon as his door was closed he heard the radio again. "Sufficient force is available to recapture the institution at any time. The question is whether the lives of twenty-eight innocent men is a weighty enough ransom to purchase amnesty for nearly two thousand convicted criminals. In the morning . . ." Farragut looked up and saw Marshack's shadow on the glass door. He slammed open a desk drawer, ripped out a ditto sheet and put it as noisily as possible into the machine. He watched the shadow of Marshack slide down the glass to where he could, crouched, see through the keyhole. Farragut shook the papers vigorously and read the messages, written in pencil in a child's scrawl. "All personnel is to show top strength in all gatherings. No strength, no gatherings." That was the first. The second read: "Louisa Pierce Spingarn, in memory of her beloved son Peter, has arranged for interested inmates to be photographed in full color beside a decorated Christmas tree and to have said photographs . . ." Marshack opened the door and stood there, the executioner, the power of endings.

"What is this, Sergeant?" Farragut asked. "What is this thing about a Christmas tree?"

"I don't know, I don't know," said Marshack. "She's a fucking do-gooder, I guess. They cause all the trouble. Efficiency is all that matters and when you don't get efficiency you get shit."

"I know," said Farragut, "but what's this all about a Christmas tree?"

"I don't know the whole story," Marshack said, "but this broad, this Spingarn, had a son who I think died in prison. Not in this country but in someplace like India or Japan. Maybe it was in some war. I don't know. So she thinks about prisons a lot and she goes to some mark in the Department of Correction and she gives them this money so that you assholes can be photographed in full color standing beside a Christmas tree and then have these pictures mailed to your families if any of you got families, which I doubt. It's a terrible waste of money."

"When did she make this arrangement?"

"Oh, I don't know. A long time ago. Years ago, maybe. Somebody just remembered about it this afternoon. It's just something to keep you assholes busy. Next thing they'll have needle-threading contests with cash prizes. Cash prizes for the boob who shits the biggest turd. Cash prizes for anything, just to keep you busy."

Marshack sat on the edge of the desk. Why, Farragut wondered, did he shave his skull? Nits? A shaved skull was associated in Farragut's mind with Prussians, cruelty and executioners. Why should a prison guard aim at this? On the evidence of his shaved skull Farragut guessed that if Marshack were on the barricades at The Wall he would gun down a hundred men with no excitement and no remorse. The shaved skulls, Farragut thought, will always be with us. They are easily recognized but impossible to alter or cure. Farragut longed fleetingly for class structures and benighted hierarchies. They could exploit the shaved heads. Marshack was stupid. Stupidity was his greatest usefulness; his vocation. He was very useful. He was indispensable at greasing machinery and splicing BX cables and he would be a courageous and fierce mercenary in some border skirmish if someone more sophisticated gave the order to attack. There would be some universal goodness in the man—he would give you a match for your cigarette and save you a seat at the movies— but there was no universality to his lack of intelligence. Marshack might respond to the sovereignty of love, but he could not master geometry and he should not be asked to. Farragut put him down as a killer.

"I'm getting out of here at four," Marshack said. "I ain't never been so anxious to get out of no place in my whole life. I'm getting out of here at four and I'm going to go home and drink a whole bottle of Southern Comfort and if I feel like it I'm going to drink another bottle and if I can't forget everything I seen and felt around here in the last couple of hours I'll drink another. I won't have to come back here until four on Monday and I'm going to be drunk all the time. Long ago when they first invented the atomic bomb people used to worry about its going off and killing everybody, but they didn't know that mankind has got enough dynamite right in his guts to tear the fucking planet to pieces. Me, I know."

"Why did you take this job?"

"I don't know why I took this job. It was my uncle told me. He was my father's older brother. My father believed everything he said. So he said I should get a peaceful job in the jailhouse, retire in twenty years on half pay and begin a new life at forty with a guaranteed income. Do anything. Open up a parking lot. Grow oranges. Run a motel. Only he didn't know that in a place like this you get so tensed up that you can't digest a Lifesaver. I threw up my lunch. We had a good meal for once—chickpeas and chicken wings—and I threw up the whole mess, right on the floor. I can't keep nothing on my stomach. Another twenty minutes and I'm walking to my car and I'm driving my car home to 327 Hudson Street and I'm getting my bottle of Southern Comfort out of the top of the closet and my glass from the kitchen and I'm going to forget everything. When you type those out put them in my office. It's the one with the plants. The door's open. Toledo'll pick them up."

He closed the glass door. The radio was dead. Farragut typed: LOUISA PIERCE SPINGARN, IN MEMORY OF HER BELOVED SON PETER, HAS ARRANGED FOR INTERESTED INMATES TO BE PHOTOGRAPHED IN FULL COLOR BESIDE A DECORATED CHRISTMAS TREE AND TO HAVE SAID PHOTOGRAPHS MAILED AT NO COST TO THE INMATE'S LOVED ONES. PICTURE-TAKING WILL BEGIN AT 900/8/27 IN THE ORDER OF RECEIVED APPLICATIONS. WHITE SHIRTS ALLOWABLE. DON'T BRING NOTHING BUT A HANDKERCHIEF.

Farragut turned off his light, closed the door and walked down the tunnel to the open door of Marshack's office. The room had three windows and it was the one, as Marshack had said, with the plants. The windows had vertical bars outside, but Marshack had put horizontal rods on the inside and many plants hung from these. There were twenty or thirty hanging plants. Hanging plants, Farragut thought, were the beloved of the truly lonely—those men and women who, burning with lust, ambition and nostalgia, watered their hanging plants. They cultivated their hanging plants and he guessed that they talked to them since they talked to everything else—doors, tables and the wind up the chimney. He recognized very few of the plants. Ferns he knew; ferns and geraniums. He picked a geranium leaf, broke it in his fingers and smelled the oil. It smelled like a geranium—the stuffy, complex perfume of some lived-in and badly ventilated interior. There were many other kinds with leaves of all shapes, some of them the color of red cabbage and some of them dull browns and yellows—not the lambent autumnal spectrum, but the same spectrum of death, fixed in the nature of the plant. He was pleased and surprised to see that the killer, narrowly confined by his stupidity, had tried to change the bleakness of the room where he worked with plants that lived and grew and died, that depended upon his attention and his kindness, that had at least the fragrance of moist soil and that in their greenness and their life stood for the valleys and pastures of milk and honey. All the plants hung from copper wire. Farragut had built radios when he was young. He remembered that a hundred feet of copper wire was the beginning of a radio set.

Farragut unhooked a plant from a curtain rod and went after the copper wire. Marshack had looped the wire through holes in the pots, but he had used the wire so generously that it would take Farragut an hour or more to get the wire he needed. Then he heard footsteps. He stood in front of the floored plant, a little frightened, but it was only Toledo. Farragut passed him the ditto sheets and gave him a strong interrogative eye. "Yeah, yeah," said Toledo. He spoke not in a whisper but in a very flat voice. "They got twenty-eight hostages. That's at least two thousand eight hundred pounds of flesh, and they can make every ounce of it sing." Toledo was gone.

Farragut returned to his desk, broke the least-used key from the typewriter, honed it on the old granite of the wall, thinking of the ice age and its contribution to the hardness of the stone. When he had the key honed to a hair edge, he went back to Marshack's office and cut the wire off eighteen plants. He put the wire in his underpants, turned off the lights and walked back up the empty tunnel. He walked clumsily with the wire in his pants and if anyone had questioned him about his limp he would have said that the shitty humid day gave him rheumatism.

"734–508–32 reporting in," he said to Tiny.

"What's the news?"

"Beginning tomorrow at nine hundred any asshole who wants to be photographed in full color standing beside a Christmas tree has got his wish."

"No shit," said Tiny.

"I'm not shitting you," said Farragut. "You'll get the announcement in the morning."

Farragut, loaded with copper wire, sat down on his cot. He would hide it under the mattress as soon as Tiny's back was turned. He unwound the toilet paper from its roll, folded the paper into neat squares and put this in his copy of Descartes. When he had made radios as a boy he had wound the wire on an oatmeal box. He guessed a toilet paper roll would be nearly as good. The bedspring would work for an aerial, the ground was the radiator, Bumpo's diamond was the diode crystal and the Stone had his earphones. When this was completed he would be able to get continuous news from The Wall. Farragut was terribly excited and highly composed. The public address system made him jump. "SHORT ARM FOR CELLBLOCK F IN TEN MINUTES. SHORT ARM FOR CELLBLOCK F IN TEN MINUTES."

Short arm was, for the calendar freaks, the first Thursday of every month. It was for the rest of them whenever it was announced. Farragut guessed that short arm, along with the Christmas tree, was a maneuver to dissipate their excitement. They would be humiliated and naked and the power of mandatory nakedness was inestimable. Short arm involved having some medical riffraff and a nurse from the infirmary examine their genitals for venereal suppuration. At the announcement there was some hooting and shouting, but not much. Farragut, with his back to Tiny, got out of his pants and put them neatly under the mattress to preserve their press. He also got rid of the copper.

The doctor, when he was let in, was wearing a full suit and a felt hat. He looked tired and frightened. The nurse was a very ugly man who was called Veronica. He must have been pretty years ago because in a dim, dim light he had the airs and graces of a youth, but in a stronger light he looked like a frog. The ardor that had rucked his face and made it repulsive still seemed to burn. These two sat down at Tiny's desk and Tiny gave them the records and unlocked the cells. Naked, Farragut could smell himself and he could also smell Tennis, Bumpo and the Cuckold. They had not had a shower since Sunday and the smell was strong and like a butcher's spoiled trimmings. Bumpo went on first. "Squeeze it," said the doctor. The doctor's voice was strained and angry. "Pull back the foreskin and squeeze it. Squeeze it, I said." The doctor's suit was cheap and stained, and so were his tie and his vest. Even his eyeglasses were soiled. He wore the felt hat to stress the sovereignty of sartorial rule. He, the civilian judge, was crowned with a hat while the penitents were naked, and with their sins, their genitals, their boastfulness and their memories exposed they seemed shameful. "Spread your cheeks," said the doctor. "Wider. Wider. Next—73482."

"It's 73483," said Tiny.

"I can't read your writing," the doctor said. "73483."

73483 was Tennis. Tennis was a sunbather and had a snowy bum. His arms and legs were, for an athlete, very thin. Tennis had clap. It was very still. For this ceremony, the sense of humor that survived even the darkness of the Valley was extinguished. Extinguished too was the convulsive gaiety Farragut had seen at chow.

"Where did you get it?" the doctor asked. "I want his name and his number." With a case in hand, the doctor seemed reasonable and at ease. He reset his eyeglasses elegantly with a single finger and then drew his spread fingers across his brow.

"I don't know," said Tennis. "I don't remember any such thing."

"Where did you get it?" the doctor said. "You'd better tell me."

"Well, it could have been during the ball game," said Tennis. "I guess it was during the ball game. Some dude blew me while I was watching the ball game. I don't know who it was. I mean if I'd known who it was

I would have killed him, but I was so interested in the game that I didn't notice. I love baseball."

"You didn't slip it up somebody's ass in the shower," said the doctor.

"Well, if I did it was by accident," said Tennis. "It was entirely by accident. We only get showers once a week and for a man, a tennis champion, who takes showers three or four times a day, when you only get into the shower once a week it's very confusing. You get dizzy. You don't know what's going on. Oh, if I knew, sir, I'd tell you. If I'd known what was going on I would have hit him, I would have killed him. That's the way I am. I'm very high-strung."

"He stole my Bible," Chicken screamed, "he stole my limp leather copy of the Holy Bible. Look, look, the sonofabitch stole my Holy Bible."

Chicken was pointing at the Cuckold. The Cuckold was standing with his knees knocked together in a ludicrous parody of feminine shyness. "I don't know what he's talking about," he said. "I ain't stole nothing of his." He made a broad gesture with his arms to demonstrate his empty-handedness. Chicken pushed him. The Bible fell from between his legs and hit the floor. Chicken grabbed the book. "My Bible, my Holy Bible, it was sent to me by my cousin Henry, the only member of my family I heard from in three years. You stole my Holy Bible. You are so low I wouldn't want to spit on you." Then he spat on the Cuckold. "I never heard, I never dreamed of anybody so low that he would steal from a man in prison a Holy Bible given to him by his loving cousin."

"I didn't want your Goddamned Bible and you know

it," roared the Cuckold. He had much more volume to his voice than Chicken and pitched it at a lower register. "You never looked at your Bible. There was about an inch of dust on it. For years I heard you talking about how the last thing in the world you needed was a Bible. For years I've been hearing you bad-mouth your cousin Henry for sending you a Bible. Everybody in the block is tired of hearing you talk about Henry and the Bible. All I wanted was the leather to make wrist-watch straps. I wasn't going to hurt the Bible. I was going to return the Bible to you without the leather was all. If you wanted to read the Bible instead of complaining about how it wasn't a can of soup, you would have found the Bible just as readable when I returned it."

"It stinks," muttered Chicken. He was holding the Bible to his nose and making loud noises of inhalation. "He stuck my Bible up under his balls. Now it stinks. The Holy Scripture stinks of his balls. Genesis, Exodus, Leviticus, Deuteronomy stink."

"Shut up, shut up," said Tiny. "The next time any of you opens your mouth you get a day's cell lock."

"But," said Chicken.

"There's one," said Tiny.

"Religious hypocrite," said the Cuckold.

"Two," said Tiny wearily.

Chicken clapped the Bible over his heart as some men put their hats over their hearts when the flag is passing by. He raised his face into the light of that late August afternoon. Tennis was crying. "Honestly I don't remember. If I could remember I'd tell you. If I'd known who it was I'd kill him."

It was a long time before the doctor gave up on

Tennis and wrote him a prescription. Then one by one the others exhibited themselves and were checked off the roster. Farragut felt hungry, and glancing at his watch, saw how late it had gotten. It was an hour past chow. Tiny and the doctor were arguing about something on the roster. Tiny had locked the cells after the Cuckold grabbed the Bible and they stood naked, waiting to get back into their cells and into their clothes.

The light in the prison, that late in the day, reminded Farragut of some forest he had skied through on a winter afternoon. The perfect diagonal of the light was cut by bars as trees would cut the light in some wood, and the largeness and mysteriousness of the place was like the largeness of some forest—some tapestry of knights and unicorns—where a succinct message was promised but where nothing was spoken but the vastness. The slanting and broken light, swimming with dust, was also the dolorous light of churches where a bereft woman with a hidden face stood grieving. But in his darling snowy forest there would be an everlasting newness in the air, and here there was nothing but the bestial goat smell of old Farragut and the gall of having been gulled. They had been gulled. They had gulled themselves. The word from The Wall—and it was known to most of them—had promised them the thrust, the strength of change, and this had been sapped by quarrels about clap and prayerbooks and wrist-watch straps.

Farragut felt impotent. No girl, no ass, no mouth could get him up, but he felt no gratitude for this cessation of his horniness. The last light of that sweaty

day was whitish, the white afterglow you see in the
windows of Tuscan paintings, an ending light but one
that seems to bring the optical nerve, the powers of
discernment, to a climax. Naked, utterly unbeautiful,
malodorous and humiliated by a clown in a dirty suit
and a dirty hat, they seemed to Farragut, in this climax
of the light, to be criminals. None of the cruelties of
their early lives—hunger, thirst and beatings—could
account for their brutality, their self-destructive thefts
and their consuming and perverse addictions. They
were souls who could not be redeemed, and while
penance was a clumsy and a cruel answer, it was some
measure of the mysteriousness of their fall. In the
white light they seemed to Farragut to be fallen men.

They dressed. It was dark. Chicken began to
scream, "Chow. Chow. Chow." Most of the others
joined in on the chant. "No chow," said Tiny. "Kitchen's
closed for repairs." "Three squares a day is our constitutional right," screamed Chicken. "We'll get a writ of
habeas corpus. We'll get twenty writs. . . ." Then he
began to shout: "TV. TV. TV." Almost everyone joined
in on this. "TV's broken," said Tiny. This lie increased
the loudness of the chanting and Farragut, weary with
hunger and everything else, found himself sinking,
with no resistance at all, into a torpor that was the
worst of his positions of retreat. Down he seemed to go,
his shoulders rounded and his neck bent, down into a
lewd and putrescent nothingness. He breathed, but that
seemed to be all he did. The din of the shouting only
made his torpor more desirable, the noises worked on
him like the blessing of some destructive drug, and he

saw his brain cells like the cells of a honeycomb being destroyed by an alien solvent. Then Chicken set fire to his mattress and began to blow on the small flames and ask men to pass him paper to keep the fire going. Farragut barely heard him. They passed up toilet paper, hoarded announcements and letters from home. Chicken blew so hard on the flames that he blew out all his teeth—uppers and lowers. When he got these back into place he began to yell—Farragut barely heard him—"Set fire to your mattress, burn the fucking place down, watch the flames leap, see them coughing to death, see the flames shoot up through the roof, see them burning, see them burning and crying." Farragut heard this remotely, but he distinctly heard Tiny pick up the phone and ask: "Red Alert." Then Tiny shouted: "Well, what the hell did you tell me you got a Red Alert for when you ain't got no Red Alert. Well, all right—I got them all yelling and throwing stuff around and setting fire to their mattresses, so why ain't my cellblock just as dangerous as C and B? Just because I ain't got no millionaires and governors in here don't mean that my cellblock ain't as dangerous as some other cellblock. I got all the boobs in here and it's like a dynamite cap. I tell you they're burning their mattresses. Well, don't tell me you got this Red Alert when you're drinking whiskey in the squad room. All right, you're scared. So am I. I'm human. I could use a drink. Well, all right, then, but step on it."

"CELL BLOCK F UNDER RED ALERT. CELL BLOCK F UNDER RED ALERT." That was ten minutes later. Then the door rolled open and they came in, eighteen of them wearing masks and yellow waterproofs, armed with clubs and gas cans. Two men got the hose off the rack and aimed it at the block. They moved clumsily. It could be the waterproofs or maybe they were drunk. Chisholm pulled off his mask and got the bullhorn. Chisholm was drunk and frightened. His features were all wrong, like a face reflected in moving water. He had the brows of one man, the mouth of another and the thin, bitter voice of a third. "Stand at attention by your doors or you'll get the hose and you'll get it like a bunch of sticks with nails in them, you'll get it like stones, you'll get it like a rod of iron. Put out your fire, Chicken, and get it through your heads that you men is powerless. This place is surrounded with armed troops from all over the state. We got the power to scatter your fire wherever you light it. You is powerless. Now put out your mattress, Chicken, and sleep in your own mess. Blow out their lights, Tiny. Sweet dreams."

They were gone, the door closed and it was dark. Chicken was whimpering. "Don't sleep, nobody, don't nobody close their eyes. You close your eyes they'll kill you. They'll kill you in your sleep. Don't nobody go to sleep."

In the blessed dark Farragut got his copper wire and his toilet paper roll and began to build his radio. How beautiful the wire seemed, a slender, clean, gold-colored tie to the world of the living, from which he seemed to hear, now and then, the clash of men, the roar of men tearing at one another's heads. It came and went and he dismissed it as an illusion, compared at least to the splendor of building, out of paper and wire, some bond or lock or shining buckle that could fasten two worlds. When it was done he sighed like a gratified lover and mumbled: "Praise be to Thee, O Lord." Chicken was still whimpering: "Don't go to sleep, nobody. Nobody goes to sleep." Farragut slept heavily.

When Farragut woke he saw through the poor light and the dark sky that the weather had not changed. A thunderstorm or a strong northwest wind might break it or it might taper off into a ten-hour rain and a slow clearing. He saw, at the window, that Chisholm had lied. There were no troops around the walls. Had there been troops there he would have heard the noise, he would have felt the stir of troops. There was nothing, and he felt disappointed. Perhaps there were no troops to spare. The heaviness of the air was depressing and he smelled worse. So did Bumpo and Tennis. A reproduction of the ditto he had typed was stuck between the bars. LOUISA PIERCE SPINGARN, IN MEMORY OF HER BELOVED SON PETER . . . The chow bell rang at seven. Goldfarb was on duty. "Single file," he shouted, "single file and ten paces between youse. Single file." They lined up at the door and when it opened, Goldfarb parceled them out at ten paces, all excepting the Stone, who had left his glass ear in the cell and couldn't be made to understand. Goldfarb shouted at him, roared at him, and raised ten fingers in the air, but the Stone only smiled and hunkered after the ass of Ransome, who was ahead. He wasn't going to be left alone, not for a minute. Goldfarb let him go. In the tunnel to the mess hall Farragut saw the precautions he had typed. ALL PERSONNEL IS TO SHOW TOP STRENGTH IN ALL GATHERINGS. All along the tunnel at regular intervals were guards in waterproofs with truncheons and gas cans. The few faces that Farragut saw seemed more haggard than the prisoners'. In the mess hall a tape was playing: "EAT STANDING UP IN YOUR PLACE IN LINE. EAT STANDING UP IN YOUR PLACE IN LINE. NO TALKING. . . ." Breakfast was tea, last night's meat scraps and a hard-boiled egg. "Coffee they don't got," a KP said. "They got nothing. Last night's delivery man leaked the news. They still got twenty-eight hostages by the balls. Amnesty they want. Pass it along. I been dishing out this shit for twelve hours. My feet are living but the rest of me's dead." Farragut wolfed his meat and his egg, dropped his tray and spoon into the dirty water and went back to his block with his neighbors. Clang. "What did the cashier say to the cash register?" said Bumpo.

"I don't know."

"I count on you, said the cashier to the cash register."

Farragut hurled himself onto his bunk and gave an impersonation of a man tormented by confinement, racked with stomach cramps and sexual backfires. He tore at his scalp with his nails, scratched his thighs and his chest and mumbled to Bumpo between groans, "Riot at The Wall. Twenty-eight hostages by the balls. Their balls equal freedom and amnesty." He howled, bucked with his pelvis and then buried his face in the pillow, under which he could feel the beginnings of his radio, safe, he guessed, because with the staff half dead, scared and thinned, he'd bet by sick call there wouldn't be any search for contraband.

"You're a great cash register," said Bumpo clearly. "Why did the raisin look sad?"

"Because he's a dried prune?" asked Farragut.

"No. Because he's a worried grape," said Bumpo.

"No talking," said Goldfarb.

Then Farragut couldn't remember what he had done with the typewriter key he had sharpened and used to cut wire. If it was found, classed as a shiv and traced back to him with fingerprints, he could get another three years. He tried to reenact all his movements in Marshack's office: he counted the plants, heard Toledo speak about the pounds of flesh, went off to his office and sharpened the key. He had cut the wire, stuffed it into his pants, but haste and anxiety obscured what he had done with the key. He had turned off the lights, limped up the tunnel and explained to someone who didn't exist that the humidity gave him rheumatism. He didn't worry about the plants and the wire—it was the key that could incriminate him. But where was the key? On the floor by a plant, stuck into some soil or left on Marshack's desk? The key, the key! He couldn't remember. He could remember that Marshack had said he wouldn't be back until four on Monday, but having said Monday he could not remember the day of the week. Yesterday had been short arm or was it the day before or the day before that when the Cuckold had swiped Chicken's Bible. He didn't know. Then Tiny relieved Goldfarb and read an announcement that opened with a date and Farragut was given the news that this was Saturday. He could worry later about the key.

Tiny announced that all inmates who wanted to be photographed should shave, dress and be ready when their turn came. Everybody on the block had signed up, even the Stone. Farragut observed the success of this maneuver. It did diffuse their explosive unrest. He guessed that a man walking to the electric chair would be happy to pick his nose. Calmly and even happily they shaved, washed their armpits, dressed and waited.

"I want to play cards with the Stone," said Ransome. "I want to play cards with the Stone."

"He don't know how to play cards," said Tiny.

"He wants to play cards," said Ransome. "Look at him." The Stone was smiling and nodding, as he would for anything. Tiny sprang Ransome, who carried his chair into the corridor and sat down opposite the Stone with a deck of cards. "One for you and one for me," he said.

Then Chicken began to strike his guitar and sing:

There is twenty-eight bottles
Hanging on the wall,
And if one of them bottles
Started to fall,
They'd be twenty-seven bottles
Hanging on the wall,
And if one of them bottles
Started to fall—

Tiny blew. "You want Chisholm in here with that bone-breaking hose crew?"

"No, no, no," said Chicken. "I don't want nothing like that. That ain't what I want. If I was on the grievance committee, whatever that is, one of the first things I'd bring up is the visiting room. Now, they tell me it's a lot better than the visiting room at The Wall, but even so, if I had some chick come in to visit me I wouldn't want to meet her over a counter like I was trying to sell her something. If some chick come in to visit me—"

"You been in here twelve years," shouted Tiny, "and you ain't never once had a visitor. Never once, not ever in twelve years."

"Maybe I had a visitor when you was on vacation," said Chicken. "Maybe I had a visitor when you had that hernia operation. You was out six weeks."

"That was ten years ago."

"Well, as I say, if some chick come to visit me I wouldn't want to have her sweet-talk me across a counter. I'd like to sit down with her at a table with an ashtray for butts and maybe offer her a soft drink."

"They got soft-drink machines."

"But at a table, Tiny, at a table. You can't have no kind of intimacy across a counter. If I could talk to my chick across this table, well, then I'd feel contented and not want to hurt nobody or start no trouble."

"In twelve years nobody come to see you. That proves that there ain't nobody on the street who knows your name. Even your own mother don't know who you are. Sisters, brothers, aunts, uncles, friends, chicks— you ain't got nothing to sit down at a table with. You is worse than dead. You shit. The dead don't shit."

Chicken began to cry then or seemed to cry, to

weep or seemed to weep, until they heard the sound of a grown man weeping, an old man who slept on a charred mattress, whose life savings in tattoos had faded to a tracery of ash, whose crotch hair was sparse and gray, whose flesh hung slack on his bones, whose only trespass on life was a flat guitar and a remembered and pitiful air of "I don't know where it is, sir, but I'll find it, sir," and whose name was known nowhere, nowhere in the far reaches of the earth or in the far reaches of his memory, where, when he talked to himself, he talked to himself as Chicken Number Two.

The chow bell rang past one and they got the order for single file at ten paces and went down the tunnel past the guards, who looked sicker. Chow was two sandwiches, one with cheese and the other with nothing but margarine. The KP was a stranger and wouldn't talk. A little after three, back in their cells, they were ordered to the education building, and single file, ten paces apart, they went there.

The education building was no longer much used. Budget cuts and a profound suspicion of the effects of education on a criminal intelligence had put out most of its lights and left it a ghostly place. On their left, unlighted, was the ghostly typewriter classroom, where eight huge, ancient and unused machines gathered dust. There were no instruments in the music room, but there was a clef, a staff and some notes drawn on the blackboard. In the dark history class, lighted only from the hall, Farragut read on the blackboard: "The new imperialism ended in 1905 to be followed by . . ." That could have been written ten or twenty years ago. The last classroom on the left was lighted and there was a stir there and over Ransome's and Bumpo's shoulders Farragut could see two bright lights on skeletal poles beamed at a plastic fir tree, blazing with ornaments. Beneath the tree were square and rectangular boxes, wrapped professionally with colored paper and brilliant ribbons. The intelligence or the craft of the hand that had set this scene filled Farragut with the deepest admiration. He listened for the clash of men, the sirens, the roar of mortal enemies, tearing at one another's heads, but this was gone, conquered by the balm of the plastic tree, glittering with crown jewels and surrounded by treasure. He imagined the figure he would cut, standing in his white shirt beside the boxes filled with cashmere sweaters, silk shirts, sable hats, needlepoint bed slippers and large jewels suitable for a man. He saw himself in the curious spectrum of color photography being taken out of an envelope by his wife and his son in the hallway at Indian Hill. He saw the rug, the table, the bowl of roses reflected in the mirror as they regarded their shame, their bad penny, their fouled escutcheon, their nemesis posed in stunning color beside a truly beautiful tree!

There was a long, battered table in the corridor, with forms to be filled out that must have been manufactured in the street by some intelligent agent. The form explained that one photograph would be mailed cost-free to a recipient designated by the inmate. The recipient should be a member of the family, but common-law wives and homosexual unions were acceptable. A second print and the negative would be delivered to Falconer, but any duplicates would be made at the inmate's own expense. Farragut printed:

"Mrs. Ezekiel Farragut. Indian Hill. Southwick, Connecticut. 06998." He printed a form for the Stone, whose name was Serafino DeMarco and whose address was in Brooklyn. Then he stepped into the brightly lighted room with the presents and the tree.

The irony of Christmas is always upon the poor in heart; the mystery of the solstice is always upon the rest of us. The inspired metaphor of the Prince of Peace and his countless lights, overwhelming the maddening and the threadbare carols, was somewhere here; here, on this asshole August afternoon the legend still had its stamina. Their motives were pure enough. Mrs. Spingarn genuinely loved her son and grieved at his cruel and unnatural end. The guards genuinely feared disorder and death. The inmates would fleetingly feel that they had a foot in the faraway street. Farragut looked above this spectacle to the rest of the classroom. There was an empty blackboard and above this an alphabet written in a Spencerian hand long, long ago. The penmanship was very elegant, with loops, hoops, tails, follow-throughs and a crossed *t* like an acrobat's bow. Above this was an American flag with forty-two stars, the white stripes dyed by time to the yellow of hot piss. One would have liked to do better, but that was the color of the flag under which Farragut had marched into battle. Then there was the photographer.

He was a slender man with a small head—a dandy, Farragut thought. His camera, on a tripod, was no bigger than a wrist-watch box, but he seemed to have a relationship with or a noticeable dependence upon the lens. He seemed to take his squinted eye away from it reluctantly. His voice was croupy and elegant. Two photographs were taken. The first was a picture of the form with the prisoner's number and the designated address. The second was of the prisoner himself, taken with a little gentle guidance. "Smile. Lift your head a little. Bring your right foot closer to your left. That's it!" When Chicken took his place and held up his form, they all read: *Mr. and Mrs. Santa Claus. Icicle Street. The North Pole.* The photographer smiled broadly and was looking around the room to share this joke with the rest of them when he suddenly grasped the solemnity of Chicken's loneliness. No one at all laughed at this hieroglyph of pain, and Chicken, sensing the stillness at this proof of his living death, swung his head around, shot up his skinny chin and said gaily, "My left profile's my best."

"That's it," said the photographer.

At his turn Farragut wondered what role to aim at, and trying to look and feel like a constant husband, a comprehensive father and a prosperous citizen, smiled broadly and stepped into the intense brightness and heat of the light. "Oh, Indian Hill," said the photographer. "I know that place. I mean I've seen the sign. Do you work there?"

"Yes," said Farragut.

"I have friends in Southwick," said the photographer. "That's it."

Farragut went to the window, where he had a broad view of cellblocks B and C. They looked, with their ranks of windows, like some obsolete Northern cotton mill. He looked in the windows for flames and a rush of shadows, but all he saw was a man hanging up his wash to dry. The passiveness of the place bewildered him. They could not all have been humiliated and gulled by nakedness and a glittering tree, but that seemed to be the case. The place seemed sleepy. Had they all retreated into the torpor he had chosen when Chicken fired his mattress? He looked again at the stranger hanging out his wash.

Farragut joined the others waiting in the corridor. Outside it had begun to rain. Ransome went among them, collecting the forms that had been photographed. These were useless and Farragut watched Ransome with interest, for he was so secretive a man that to follow any of his consecutive movements promised to be revealing. What he did, when he had collected a dozen forms, was to climb onto a chair. Ransome was a big man and the chair was rickety and he checked his safety by shifting his weight. When he felt secure he began to tear the forms into small pieces and cast them, like a sower, over the heads and shoulders of the others. His face was beaming and he sang "Silent Night." The Cuckold picked up a good bass, and considering the distance they had all come from caroling, they formed a small, strong choir, singing enthusiastically about the Virgin. The old carol and the scraps of paper falling softly through the air onto their heads and shoulders was not at all a bitter recollection on that suffocating rainy day, but a light-hearted memory of some foolishness, linked to a fall of snow.

Then they lined up and marched out. Another group of inmates stood lined up in the tunnel, waiting their turn to be photographed beside the tree. Farragut regarded them with the pleasure and surprise with which one regards the crowd waiting to get into the next show at a movie. That was the end to his cheerfulness. As soon as they saw the faces of the guards in the tunnel they saw that their Christmas was over.

Farragut washed himself carefully and vigorously with cold water and then smelled himself like a canine, sniffed his armpits and his crotch, but he couldn't tell whether it was he or Bumpo who smelled. Walton was on duty, studying his texts. He was taking a night course in automobile salesmanship. He couldn't pay too much attention to whether or not they talked. When Ransome asked to play cards with the Stone, he sprang him impatiently. "I'm studying for an exam. I'm studying for an exam. I know that none of youse knows what that means, but if I flunk this exam I got to take the whole year over again. This whole place is gone crazy. I can't study at home. The baby's sick and crying all the time. I come here early to study in the squad room, but the squad room is like an insane asylum. Now I come here looking for peace and quiet and it's like the Tower of Babel. Play cards but shut up."

Farragut, taking advantage of this, began to shout at Bumpo. "Why the fuck don't you wash your skin? I've washed myself, I've washed myself all over, but I can't enjoy my clean smell because you smell like a waste can in the back alley behind some butcher store."

"Oh, I do, do I!" yelled Bumpo. "So that's how you get your rocks off, sniffing cans outside butchers'."

"Shut up, shut up, shut up," said Walton. "I got to study for this exam. You know what it's like, Farragut. If I fail this exam I have to spend another year, another semester anyhow, sitting on my ass on a hard chair studying what I already knew but forgot. And my professor is a bitch. Talk if you have to, but talk softly."

"Oh, Bumpo, oh, Bumpo, dear Bumpo, darling Bumpo," said Farragut softly, "what did the cashier say to the cash register?"

"I'm a wrinkled grape," said Bumpo.

"Oh, darling Bumpo," said Farragut softly. "I have a great favor to ask of you. The history of modern civilization depends upon your arriving at an intelligent decision. I have heard you speak fluently about your willingness to give your diamond to some starving child or some lonely crone, by-passed by the thoughtless world. Now a much greater opportunity is about to be placed in your hands. I possess the rudiments of a radio—an aerial, a ground and a copper-wire tuner. All I need is an earphone and a diode crystal. The Stone has one and you have the other. With this, with your diamond, the Gordian knot of communications that threatens the Department of Correction and the government itself can be cut. They have twenty-eight hostages by the balls. A single mistake on the part of our brothers will have us cut down by the hundreds. A crucial mistake on the part of the Department of Correction may detonate riots in every prison in this nation and perhaps the world. We are millions, Bumpo, we are millions, and if our riots are triumphant we can rule the world, although you and I, Bumpo, know that we lack the brains for this. So, lacking the brainpower, the best we can hope for is a truce, and it all depends on your rock."

"Take your little prick and go home," said Bumpo softly.

"Bumpo, Bumpo, dear Bumpo, God gave you your diamond and God means you should give it to me. It is the balance, Bumpo, upon which the lives of millions depend. The radio was invented by Guglielmo Marconi in 1895. It was the beautiful discovery of that fact that electrified airwaves, containing sound, can, at a distance, be reconverted into intelligible sound. With the help of your diamond, Bumpo, we can learn exactly how much they're twisting those twenty-eight balls at The Wall."

"Fifty-six," said Bumpo.

"Thank you, Bumpo, sweet Bumpo, but if we learn this we will learn how to play our own strategies to our greatest advantage, perhaps even to buy our freedom. With your diamond I can make a radio."

"If you're such a great magician, why can't you get your ass out of here?" said Bumpo.

"I'm talking about airwaves, Bumpo, not flesh and blood. Air. Sweet air. Thin air. Do you hear me? I wouldn't be able to speak to you softly and with patience at this point if I did not believe that mathematics and geometry are a lying and a faulty analogy for the human disposition. When one finds in men's nature, as I do in yours, some convexity, it is a mistake to expect a corresponding concavity. There is no such thing as an isosceles man. The only reason I continue to plead with you, Bumpo, is my belief in the inestimable richness of human nature. I want your diamond to save the world."

Bumpo laughed. His laughter was genuine and boyish and loud and ringing. "You're the first dude to spring that one on me. That's a new one. Save mankind. All I said was I was going to save some hungry little kid or some old person. I didn't say nothing about the world. It's worth anywhere from nineteen to twenty-six thousand. The diamond's hard but the market ain't. They'd have chopped off my finger years ago if the stone wasn't too big to fence. It's a big, safe stone. I never had an offer like yours. I had twenty-seven offers, maybe more. I been offered every cock in the place, of course, and every asshole, but I can't eat cock and I don't like asshole. I don't mind a nice hand job, but no hand job is worth twenty-six thousand. Years ago there was a guard, he got fired, who offered me a case of whiskey once a week. All kinds of shit like that. Outside food. Tons of it. Also a lifetime supply of cigarettes for a chain smoker. Lawyers. They stand in line to talk with me. They promise me retrials, guaranteed pardons and dismissals. There was one guard who offered me an escape. I was going to go out on the underchassis of a delivery truck. That's the only one that really interested me. This truck was coming in on Tuesdays and Thursdays and he knew the driver, the driver was his brother-in-law. So he rigged up this hammock under the chassis, it was just big enough to hold me. He showed me the whole thing and I even practiced getting into it, but he wanted the rock before I got out. Of course I wouldn't give it to him and the whole thing blew up. But nobody ever told me I could save the world." He looked at his diamond and turned it, smiling at the fire it contained. "You didn't know you could save the world, did you?" he asked the diamond.

"Oh, why would anyone want to get out of a nice

place like this?" asked Chicken. He struck some chords on his guitar and while he went on talking in his bluegrass voice his song was unaccompanied. "Who would want to riot in order to get out of a nice place like this? In the paper now you read there's unemployment everywhere. That's why the lieutenant governor is in here. He can't get no job outside. Even famous movie stars with formerly millions is standing in line with their coat collars turned up around their necks waiting for a handout, waiting for a bowl of that watery bean soup that don't keep you from feeling hungry and makes you fart. Out in the street everybody's poor, everybody's out of work and it rains all the time. They mug one another for a crust of bread. You have to stand in line for a week just to be told you ain't got no job. We stand in line three times a day to get our nice minimal-nutritional hot meal, but out in the street they stand in line for eight hours, twenty-four hours, sometimes they stand in line for a lifetime. Who wants to get out of a nice place like this and stand in line in the rain? And when they ain't standing in line in the rain they worry about atomic war. Sometimes they do both. I mean they stand in line in the rain and worry about atomic war because if there's an atomic war they'll all be killed and find themselves standing in line at the gates of hell. That's not for us, men. In case of an atomic war we'll be the first to be saved. They got bomb shelters for us criminals all over the world. They don't want us loose in the community. I mean they'll let the community burn before they'll set us free, and that will be our salvation, friends. They'd rather burn than have us running around the streets, because everybody knows that we eat babies, fuck old women up the ass and burn down hospitals full of helpless cripples. Who would ever want to get out of a nice place like this?"

"Hey, Farragut, come down and play cards with the Stone," said Ransome. "Let Farragut out, will you, Walton? The Stone wants to play cards with Farragut."

"I will if you'll shut up," said Walton. "I got to pass this exam. You promise to shut up?"

"We promise," said Ransome.

Farragut's cell door opened and he went down the block to the Stone's, carrying his chair. The Stone was smiling like a fool, which he may have been. The Stone handed him the pack of cards and he dealt them out, saying, "One for you and one for me." Then he fanned out his hand, but that many cards were bulky and a dozen fell to the floor. When he stopped to pick them up he heard a voice, not a whisper but a normal voice, tuned to a minimum volume. It was the Glass Ear—the two-hundred-dollar hearing aid—tuned to a radio frequency. He saw the four batteries in their canvas-covered corset lying on the floor and the plastic, flesh-colored orifice from which he guessed the voice came. He picked up his cards and began to slap them out on a table, saying, "One for you and one for me." The voice said, "Registration for continuing education classes in conversational Spanish and cabinetmaking will be open from five to nine on Monday through Friday at the Benjamin Franklin High School, situated on the corner of Elm and Chestnut Streets." Then Farragut heard piano music. It was the dreariest of the Chopin preludes—that prelude they use in murder films before the shot is fired; that prelude that was expected to evoke for men of his day and earlier the image of a little girl with braids, confined for some cruel hour to a bleak room, where she was meant to produce the bleat of impuissant waves and the sad stir of falling leaves. "The latest news from The Wall, or the Amana Prison," said the voice, "is that negotiations are still proceeding between the administration and the committee of inmates. Forces to secure the institution are available, but reports of impatience among the troops have been denied. Five of the hostages have testified on radio and TV that they have been receiving food, medical supplies and adequate protection under the leadership of the Black Muslim faction. The governor has made it clear for the third time that he does not have the power to grant amnesty. A final petition for the release of the hostages has been presented and the inmates will give their answer at daybreak tomorrow. Daybreak is officially slated for six twenty-eight, but the weather predictions are for cloudy skies and more rain. In the local news, an octogenarian bicyclist named Ralph Waldo won the Golden Age Bicycle Race in the town of Burnt Valley on his eighty-second birthday. His time was one hour and eighteen minutes. Congratulations, Ralph! Mrs. Charles Roundtree of Hunters Bridge in the northeast corner of the state claims to have seen an unidentified flying object at such a close range that the draft raised her skirts while she was hanging out the wash. Stay tuned for details of the five-alarm fire in Tappansville." Then another voice sang:

Garroway toothpaste cleans your teeth,
Both the dirt above and the dirt beneath,
Garroway toothpaste cavities hate,
Garroway toothpaste is for you and your mate.

Farragut slapped down cards for another ten minutes and then began to shout, "I got a toothache. I want to quit. I got a toothache."

"Go home, go home," said Walton. "I got to study."

Farragut picked up his chair, and stopping by Ransome's cell, he said, "I got this terrible toothache. It's a wisdom tooth. I'm forty-eight years old and I still got my wisdom teeth. This one on the left is just like a clock. It starts aching at around nine at night and stops at dawn. Dawn tomorrow is when I'll know whether the pain is over, whether or not the tooth has to come out. I'll know at daybreak. That's about six twenty-eight."

"Thank you, Miss America," said Ransome.

Farragut stumbled back to his cell, got into bed and slept.

He had a dream that was unlike the day. His dream was in the most vivid colors, those aniline dyes that the eye receives only after this spectrum has been extracted by a camera. Farragut is on a cruise ship, experiencing a familiar mixture of freedom, boredom and sunburn. He swims in the pool, drinks with the international crowd in the bar at noon, gets laid during the siesta, plays deck tennis, paddle tennis, and is in and out of the pool and back in the bar at four. He is all limber, ballsy and turning a golden hue that will be wasted in the dark bars and clubs where he will lunch on his return. So he is idle and a little uneasy with his idleness when, one afternoon at the end of the siesta, a schooner is seen coming up from the port side. The schooner flies some flags, but he does not understand these. He does notice that the cruiser has reduced her speed. The wave at the bow grows smaller and smaller and then there is none and the schooner sails alongside the towering ship.

The schooner has come for him. He goes below, climbs down a rope ladder onto her deck and as they sail away he waves goodbye to his friends on the cruise —men, women and the members of the ship's orchestra. He does not know who owns the schooner and who greets him there. He remembers nothing except that he stands on her deck and watches the cruise ship regain speed. She is a big old-fashioned cruiser, named for a queen, white as a bride, with three canted stacks and a little gold lace, like a toy boat, at her bow. She goes crazily off course, veers to port and heads at full tilt for a nearby island that looks like one of the Atlantic islands, only with palms. She rams the beach, heels to starboard and bursts into flame, and while he sails away he can see, over his shoulder, the pyre and the enormous column of smoke. The instant he woke, the brightness of the dream's colors were quenched by the grayness of Falconer.

Farragut woke. He swung his head from his watch to the window. It was six twenty-eight. Rain was falling into that part of the world and he guessed into The Wall. It was Tiny who had waked him. "Reach for a Lucky instead of a sweet," said Tiny. "Chesterfields, they satisfy. I'd walk a mile for a Camel." He had five cigarettes in his hand. Farragut took two. They were loosely rolled and were, he guessed, cannabis. He looked lovingly at Tiny, but any fondness or love he felt for the guard fell way short of Tiny's haggardness. His eyes were red. The lines from his nostrils past his mouth were like the ruts in a dirt road and there was no life or responsiveness left in his countenance. He stumbled down the block, saying, "Reach for a Lucky instead of a sweet. I'd walk a mile for a Camel." The old cigarette mottoes were older than either of them. Everyone but the Stone knew what they had and what to do and Ransome helped the Stone. "Suck on it and hold it in your lungs." Farragut lighted his first, sucked on the smoke, held it in his lungs and felt the true, the precious amnesty of the drug spread through his frame. "Wow," he said. "Hot shit," said Chicken. There was groaning all over the place. Tiny bumped into the cell edge and bumped his arm. "There's more where that came from," he said. He fell into his steel chair, buried his head in his arms and began to snore.

The amnesty on which Farragut exhaled formed a cloud—a gray cloud like the clouds that could begin to be seen outside his window—and raised him nicely off his earthbound cot, raised him above all earthly things. The noise of the rain seemed to be a gentleness—something his bellicose mother, pumping gas in her opera cloak, had missed. Then he heard the squeek-geek-growl of the Stone's glass ear and some sleepy urging from Ransome. "Jiggle it, jiggle it, jiggle it, for Christ's sake." Then he heard the voice of a woman, not, he thought in the expansiveness of cannabis, the voice of a young woman or an old one, neither the voice of beauty nor of plainness—the voice of a woman who might sell you a package of cigarettes anywhere in the world.

"Hi, people! This is Patty Smith, anchorwoman for Eliot Hendron, who, as you may not know, has been overwhelmed by the events of the last half hour. The Wall has been repossessed by state troops. The administration petition with a plea for further time was burned by the inmates' committee at six A.M. The inmates agreed to the plea for further time but to nothing else. There appear to have been preparations for the execution of the hostages. The gas attack began at six-eight, followed two minutes later by the order to fire. Firing lasted six minutes. It is too early to estimate the number of the dead, but Eliot, my partner and the last eyewitness in yard K, estimated them as at least fifty dead and fifty dying. Troopers have stripped the living of their clothes. They now lie naked in the rain and the mud, vomiting from the effects of CS-2. Excuse me, ladies and gentlemen, excuse me." She was crying. "I guess I'll have to join Eliot in the infirmary."

"Sing us a song, Chicken Number Two," said Ransome. "Oh, sing us a song."

There was a wait while Chicken shook off a little of the cannabis, reached for his guitar and struck four strong chords. Then he began to sing. His voice was reedy, sophisticated in its bluegrass flatness, but flat and reedy, it had the coarse grain of bravery. He sang:

If the only song I can sing is a sad song,
I ain't going to sing at all.

If the only song I can sing is a sad song,
I ain't going to sing at all.
I ain't going to sing about the dead and the dying,
I ain't going to sing about the knives and the firing,
I ain't going to sing about the praying and the crying—
If the only song I can sing is a sad song,
I ain't going to sing no more.

So they were naked again or nearly so, waiting in line to get new DC issue, choosing their places in front of signs that said EXTRA LARGE, LARGE, MEDIUM and SMALL, having stripped themselves of their prison grays and tossed these into a bin. The new issue was a noncommittal green, scarcely, thought Farragut, a verdant green, scarcely the green of Trinity and the long summer months, but a shade up from the gray of the living dead. It was only Farragut who sang a bar of "Greensleeves" and only the Cuckold who smiled. Considering the solemnity of this change of color, skepticism and sarcasm would have seemed to them all trifling and contemptible, for it was for this light-greenness that the men of Amana had died or had lain, vomiting and naked, for hours in the mud. That was a fact. After the revolution, discipline was less rigorous and their mail was not scrutinized, but their labor was still worth half a package of cigarettes a day and this change of uniform was the biggest thing to have been accomplished by the riot at The Wall. None of them would be so stupid as to say "Our brothers died for this," and almost none of them were so stupid as not to guess at the incalculable avarice involved in changing the dress of the prison population at a universal cost and for the profit of a handful of men who could spend a longer time snorkeling in the Lesser Antilles or getting blown on yachts or whatever they liked. There was a marked solemnity to this change of dress.

The change of dress was part of an atmosphere of amnesty that had settled over Falconer after the rebellion at The Wall had been crushed. Marshack had hung up his plants again with the wire that Farragut had stolen and no one had found the honed typewriter key. After new uniforms were issued, alterations were in order. Most of the men wanted their new issue cut and resewn along sharp lines. It was four days before there was any green thread for sale, and the supply ran out in an hour, but Bumpo and Tennis, both of whom could sew, got a spool and a week was spent in fittings and alterations. "Knock, knock," said the Cuckold, and Farragut asked him in although he did not and never had truly wanted to see his mate. He did want to hear a voice other than TV, and to feel in his cell the presence of another man, a companion. The Cuckold was a compromise, but he had no choice. The Cuckold had had his new issue cut so tight that it must be painful. The seat of his pants would bark his asshole like the saddle of a racing bike and the crotch definitely gave him pain, Farragut could see, because he flinched when he sat down. In spite of all this pain, thought Farragut uncharitably, there was nothing appetizing to be seen, but then his thinking about the Cuckold was generally uncharitable. As his mate sat down and prepared to talk again about his wife, Farragut thought that the Cuckold had an inflatable ego. He seemed, preparing to talk, to be in the act of being pumped up with gas. Farragut had the illusion that this increase in size was palpable and that the Cuckold, swelling, would push the copy of Descartes off the table, push the table up against the bars, uproot the toilet and destroy the cot where he lay. His story, Farragut knew, would be un-savory, but what Farragut didn't know was what impor-tance to give unsavory matters. They existed, they were invincible, but the light they threw was, he thought, unequal to their prominence. The Cuckold claimed to have a rich lode of information, but the facts he pos-sessed only seemed to reinforce Farragut's ignorance, suspiciousness and his capacity for despair. These were all parts of his disposition and might, he guessed, need cultivation. Haste and impetuous optimism could be contemptible, and with this in mind he did not protest when the Cuckold cleared his throat and said, "If you was to ask my advice about marriage, I would advise you not to put too much attention on fucking. I guess I married her because she was a great fuck—I mean she was my size, she came at the right time, it was great there for years. But then when she started fucking everybody, I didn't know what to do. I couldn't get any advice from the church and all I could get out of the law was that I should divorce her, but what about the kids? They didn't want me to go, even when they knew what she was doing. She even talked with me about it. When I complained about her screwing everybody, she gave me this lecture about how it wasn't an easy life. She said sucking every cock on the street was a very lonely and dangerous way to live. She told me it took courage. She did, really. She gave me this lecture. She said that in the movies and in the books you read it's a very nice and easy thing, but she'd had to face all sorts of problems. She told me about this time when I was on the road and she went to this bar and restaurant for dinner with some friends. In North Dakota we have these food divorcement laws where you eat in one place and drink in another, and she had moved from the drinking place to the eating place. But at the bar there was this very, very beautiful man. She gave him the horny eye through the doorway and he gave it right back to her. You know what I mean. The horny eye?

"So then she told me that she told her friends, very loudly, that she wasn't going to have any dessert, that she was going to drive home to her empty house and read a book. She said all this so he could hear her and would know that there wasn't going to be any husband or kids around. She knew the bartender and the bartender would give him her address. So she went home and put on a wrapper and then the doorbell rang and there he was. So right in the hallway he began to kiss her and put her hand on his cock and drop his pants, right in the front hallway, and at about this time she discovered that while he was very beautiful, he was also very dirty. She told me that he couldn't have had a bath in a month. As soon as she got a whiff of him she cooled off and began to figure out how she could get him into a shower. So he went on kissing her and getting out of his clothes and smelling worse and worse and then she suggested that maybe he would like a bath. So then he suddenly got angry and said that he was looking for a cunt, not a mother, that his mother told him when he needed a bath, that he didn't go around looking for sluts in saloons in order to be told when he needed a bath and when to get his hair cut and when to brush his teeth. So he got dressed and went away and she told me this to illustrate how to be a round heels takes all kinds of courage.

"But I did lousy things too. When I came off the road once I said hello and went upstairs to take a crap and while I was sitting there I noticed that there was this big pile of hunting and fishing magazines beside the toilet. So then I finished and pulled up my pants and came out shouting about this constipated fisherman she was fucking. I yelled and yelled. I said it was just her speed to pick up with a boob who couldn't cast a fly or take a shit. I said I could imagine him sitting there, his face all red, reading about catching the gamy muskallonge in stormy northern waters. I said that was just what she deserved, that just by looking at her I could tell it was her destiny to get reamed by one of those pimply gas pumpers who do their fishing in magazines and can't cut a turd. So she cried and cried and about an hour later I remembered that I had sub-

scribed to all these hunting and fishing magazines and
when I said that I was sorry she really didn't care and I
felt shitty." Farragut said nothing—he seldom said
anything to the Cuckold—and the Cuckold went back to
his cell and turned up his radio.

Ransome came down with the flux one Tuesday
morning and by Wednesday afternoon everyone but the
Stone had it. Chicken claimed that it came from the
pork they had been eating all week. He claimed that a
fly had flown out of his meat. He claimed to have
captured the fly and offered to show it to anyone who
asked, but no one asked. They all put in for sick call,
but Walton or Goldfarb announced that the infirmary
was overworked and that no doctor's or nurse's appointment could be made for ten days. Farragut had
the flux and a fever and so did everyone else. On
Thursday morning they were issued, in their cells, a
large dose of paregoric, which granted them an hour's
amnesty from Falconer but seemed powerless before
the flux. On Friday afternoon there was this announcement over the PA. "A PREVENTIVE VACCINE FOR THE
SPREAD OF INFLUENZA THAT HAS REACHED EPIDEMIC
PROPORTIONS IN SOME CITIES OF THE NORTHEAST
WILL BE ADMINISTERED TO REHABILITATION FACILITY
INMATES FROM THE HOURS OF NINE HUNDRED TO
EIGHTEEN HUNDRED. WAIT FOR YOUR CELL CALL. THE
INOCULATION IS MANDATORY AND NO SUPERSTITIOUS
OR RELIGIOUS SCRUPLES WILL BE RESPECTED."

"They're trying to use us as guinea pigs," said
Chicken. "We're being used as guinea pigs. I know all
about it. There was a man in here who had laryngitis.
They had this new medicine for him, this needle, they

gave it to him two, three days and they couldn't get him out of here up to the infirmary before he was dead. Then they had this guy with clap, a light case of clap, and they gave him inoculations and his balls swole up, they swole up as big as basketballs, they swole and swole so he couldn't walk and they had to take him out of here on a board with these big globes sticking up in the sheet. And then there was this guy whose bones were leaking, the marrow was leaking out of his bones which made him very weak, and so they give him these shots, these experimental shots, and he turned to stone, he turned to stone, didn't he, Tiny? Tiny, tell that's true about the fellow whose bones leaked and who turned to stone."

"Tiny ain't here," said Walton. "Tiny don't come in until Saturday."

"Well, Tiny will tell you when he comes in. He turned to stone. He was just like cement—stone. Tiny carved his initials on his ass. He turned into rock right before our eyes. And the crazies. If they think you're crazy they give you this green shot—yellowish-green, it is—and if it don't work it makes you so crazy you wouldn't believe it. Like there was this guy claimed he could play the national anthem on his toenails—all day long he did this—and then they gave him this experimental shot. Well, first he tore off part of one of his ears—I forget which side—and then stuck his fingers into his eyes and blinded himself. Tiny, isn't that true, isn't that true, Tiny, about the yellowish-green stuff they give the crazies?"

"Tiny ain't here," said Walton. "He don't come in until Saturday and I got no patience with any of you. I got a wife and a baby at home and they need this vaccine but I can't get none for them. You get medicine that millionaires can't buy and all you do is complain."

"Oh, what the hell," said Chicken. "I'll take anything they give me it's free, but I ain't no guinea pig."

They got their vaccine on Saturday afternoon—not at the infirmary but in the supply room from the windows marked EXTRA LARGE, LARGE, MEDIUM and SMALL. Fifteen or twenty men from that lot whose religious beliefs forbade them to take medicine were corralled by the used-clothes bin and Farragut asked himself if he possessed any religious beliefs for which he would endure solitary. There was his spiritual and his chemical dependence upon drugs, for which he would likely have killed a man. He realized then and only then that he had been given no methadone during the three days of the revolution and the three days of the plague. He did not understand at all. One of the orderlies giving the shots was the man who had given him methadone. When Farragut rolled up his sleeve and presented his arm for the needle, he asked, "Why haven't I been getting my methadone? It's against the law. It says right in my sentence that I'm entitled to methadone." "You're a dumb sonofabitch," said the orderly kindly. "Some of us have been wondering when you'd notice. You've been on placebos for nearly a month. You're clean, my friend, you're clean." He gave Farragut the needle and he shook a little at this extraneous and unnatural pain and imagined the vaccine coursing through his blood. "It can't be true," said Farragut, "it can't be true." "Count the days," said the orderly, "just count the days. Move along." Farragut was stunned. He went over to the door, where Chicken was waiting. Farragut's singular smallness of mind was illustrated by the fact that he resented that the Department of Correction had been successful where the three blue-ribbon drug cures he had taken had failed. The Department of Correction could not be right. He could not congratulate himself on having mastered his addiction, since he had not been aware of it. Then an image of his family, his hated origins, loomed up in his mind. Had that antic cast—that old man in his catboat, that woman pumping gas in her opera cloak, his pious brother—had they conveyed to him some pure, crude and lasting sense of perseverance? "I made a big decision," said Chicken, hooking his arm in Farragut's. "I made a very big decision. I'm going to sell my gitfiddle." Farragut felt only the insignificance of Chicken's decision in the light of what he had just been told; that, and the fact that Chicken's hold on his arm seemed desperate. Chicken seemed truly feeble and old. Farragut could not tell him that he was clean. "Why are you selling your gitfiddle, Chicken?" he asked. "Why are you going to do a thing like that?" "Three guesses," said Chicken. Farragut had to put an arm around him to get him up the slope of the tunnel and into the block.

It was very quiet. Farragut's fever reminded him of the bliss of drugs, something he seemed to have forsworn. He was torpid. Then a strange thing happened. He saw, at the open door of his cell, a young man with summery hair and immaculate clericals, holding a little tray with a silver chalice and ciborium. "I've come to celebrate the Holy Eucharist," he said. Farragut got out of bed. The stranger came into the cell. He had a very cleanly smell, Farragut noticed as he approached him and asked, "Shall I kneel?" "Yes, please," said the priest. Farragut knelt on the worn concrete, that surface of some old highway. The thought that these might be intended for his last rites did not disconcert him. There was nothing on his mind at all and he entered, completely, into the verbal pavane he had been taught as a youth. "Holy, Holy, Holy," he said in a loud and manly voice. "Heaven and earth are full of Thy Glory. Praise be to Thee, O Lord most high." When he had been blessed with the peace that passes all understanding, he said, "Thank you, Father," and the priest said, "God bless you, my son." But when the youth had left his cell and the block, Farragut began to shout, "Now, who in hell was that, Walton? Who in hell was that?"

"It was some do-gooder," said Walton. "I have to study."

"But how did he get in? I didn't ask for a priest. He didn't do his thing for anybody else. Why did he pick on me?"

"This place is going to hell," said Walton. "No wonder they got riots. They let anybody in. Salesmen. Encyclopedias. Frying pans. Vacuum cleaners."

"I'll write the governor," said Farragut. "If we can't get out, why can everybody get in here? They take your picture, they give you the Holy Eucharist, they ask your mother's maiden name."

He woke late that night. The toilet woke him. He didn't check the time. Naked, he went to his window. Bright lights burned on the drive. A station wagon with its motor running was parked in front of the main entrance. A ski rack was lashed to the roof. Then he saw two men and a woman come down the stairs. All three wore tennis sneakers. They carried an old-fashioned wooden coffin with a cross painted on its top. It was built to fit some rudimentary concept of a Byzantine male, with broad, sloping shoulders and a slender base. Whatever it contained weighed almost nothing. Lightly they lifted it onto the ski rack, secured it there and drove away. Farragut returned to bed and slept.

On Sunday afternoon when he came on duty Tiny brought Farragut half a dozen tomatoes and asked him to take Chicken into his cell. The old man needed care. Tiny explained that the infirmary was full of beds, they had put beds in the waiting room, the administration office and the corridors, but there was still no room. Farragut ate his tomatoes and agreed. Farragut made his bed in the upper bunk and Tiny got sheets and a blanket and made a bed for Chicken. When Tiny brought Chicken down the corridor he seemed half asleep and he was very smelly. "I'll wash him before I put him in clean sheets," said Farragut. "It's up to you," said Tiny. "I'm going to wash you," he said to Chicken. "You don't have to do this," said Chicken, "but I couldn't walk to the shower." "I know, I know." He drew a basin of water, got a cloth and removed the invalid shift Chicken was wearing.

The famous tattooing, on which he had squandered the fortune he had made as a brilliant second-story worker, began very neatly at his neck, like a well-cut sweater. All the colors had fled and even the blue of the primary design had gone to gray. What a gaudy sight he must have been! His chest and his upper abdomen were occupied by the portrait of a horse named Lucky Bess. On his left arm there was a sword, a shield, a serpent and the legend "Death Before Dishonor." Below this was "Mother," wreathed in flowers. On his right arm was a lewd dancer, who could probably buck when he flexed his biceps. She stood above the heads of a crowd that covered his forearm. Most of his back was a broad mountainous landscape with a rising sun, and below this, forming an arch above his buttocks, Farragut read, in faded and clumsy Gothic lettering: "Abandon all hope, ye who enter here." Serpents sprang from his groin and wound down both his legs, with his toes for fangs. All the rest of him was dense foliage. "Why did you sell your gitfiddle, Chicken?" he asked. "For two cartons of menthos," said Chicken. "But why—why?" "Curiosity killed the cat," said Chicken. "Why did you kill your brother, Zeke?"

The accident or what they called the murder had taken place, Farragut thought, because of the fact that whenever he remembered or dreamed about his family he always saw them from the back. They were always stamping indignantly out of concert halls, theaters, sports arenas and restaurants, and he, as the youngest, was always in the rear. "If Koussevitzky thinks I'll listen to that . . ." "That umpire is crooked." "This play is degenerate." "I don't like the way that waiter looked at me." "That clerk was impudent." And so on. They saw almost nothing to its completion, and that's the way he remembered them, heading, for some reason in wet raincoats, for the exit. It had occurred to him that they may have suffered terribly from claustrophobia and disguised this weakness as moral indignation.

They were also very bountiful, especially the ladies. They were always raising money to buy skinny chickens for people who lived in tenements or organizing private schools that often went bankrupt. Farragut supposed they did some good, but he had always found their magnanimity painfully embarrassing and he knew for a fact that some of the people who lived in tenements had no use for their skinny chickens. Farragut's only brother, Eben, possessed both of the family traits. He found most waiters, barmen and clerks impertinent, and to meet him for lunch in a restaurant almost always meant a scene. Eben didn't distribute chickens, but he had informed Farragut that on Saturday morning he read to the blind at the Twin Brooks Nursing Home. On this Saturday Farragut and Marcia drove out to the country where Eben and Carrie lived. It had been more than a year since the brothers had met. Farragut thought his brother heavy and even gross. The lives of his two children were tragic and Farragut resented the fact that Eben claimed these tragedies to be merely the nature of life. When they arrived Eben was about to leave for the nursing home and Farragut went along with his only brother.

The Twin Brooks Nursing Home was a complex of one-story buildings with such a commanding view of some river and some mountains that Farragut wondered if this vastness would console or embitter the dying. The heat when they stepped into the place was suffocating, and as Farragut followed his brother down the hall he noticed how heavily perfumed was the over-heated air. One after another he smelled, with his long nose, imitations of the thrilling fragrances of spring and verdancy. Pine drifted out of the toilets. The parlors smelled of roses, wisteria, carnations and lemons. But all this was so blatantly artificial that one could imagine the bottles and cans in which the scents were stored, standing on shelves in some closet.

The dying—and that's what they were—were emaciated.

"Your group is waiting in the Garden Room," a male nurse told Eben. His black hair was gleaming, his face was sallow and he gave Farragut the eye like the hustler he was. The room they entered was labeled the Garden Room presumably because the furniture was iron and painted green and reminiscent of gardens. The wall was papered with a garden landscape. There were eight patients. They were mostly in wheelchairs. One of them maneuvered on a walker. One of them was not only blind, but her legs had been amputated at the thigh. Another blind woman was very heavily rouged. Her cheeks were blazing. Farragut had seen this in old women before and he wondered if it was an eccentricity of age—although she couldn't have seen what she was doing.

"Good morning, ladies and gentlemen," said Eben. "This is my brother Zeke. We will continue to read *Romola* by George Eliot. Chapter Five. 'The Via de' Bardi, a street noted in the history of Florence, lies in Oltrarno, or that portion of the city which clothes the southern bank of the river. It extends from the Ponte Vecchio to the Piazza de' Mozzi at the head of the Ponte alle Grazie; its right-hand line of houses and walls being backed by the rather steep ascent which in the fifteenth century was known as the hill of Bogoli, the famous stone-quarry whence the city got its pavement—of dangerously unstable consistence when penetrated by rains . . .' "

The blind were very inattentive. The rouged woman fell asleep and snored lightly, but she snored. The amputee wheeled herself out of the room after a page or two. Eben went on reading to the near-dead, the truncated, the blind and the dying. Considering Farragut's passion for blue sky, he thought his brother contemptible; although they looked enough like one another to be taken for twins. Farragut did not like to look at his brother and he kept his eyes on the floor. Eben read to the end of the chapter and as they were leaving Farragut asked him why he had chosen *Romola*.

"It was their choice," said Eben.

"But the red one fell asleep," said Farragut.

"They often do," he said. "One doesn't, this late in life, blame them for anything. One doesn't take offense."

On the drive home Farragut sat as far from his brother as possible. Marcia opened the door. "Oh, I'm terribly sorry, Eben," she said, "but your wife is very upset. We were talking about the family and something she remembered or something I said made her cry."

"She cries all the time," said Eben. "Don't pay any attention to her. She cries at parades, rock music; last year she cried through the whole World Series. Don't take it seriously, don't blame yourself. Do sit down and let me get you a drink."

Marcia's face was pale. She saw the tragic household, Farragut knew, much more clearly than he. Eben was working at that time as a paid executive for some charitable foundation that carried on the tradition of distributing skinny chickens. His marriage could be dismissed, if one were that superficial, as an extraordinary sentimental and erotic collision. There were the lives of the two children to be considered, and their lives seemed ruined by the reverberations of this matrimonial crash. The young man, Eben's only son, was serving a two-year sentence in the Cincinnati workhouse for his part in some peace demonstration against some war. Rachel, the daughter, had tried three times to kill herself. Farragut had exorcised the details, but they would be remembered by Marcia. Rachel had first gone into the attic with a quart of vodka, twenty Seconals and one of those dry-cleaner's bags that threaten suffocation. She had been rescued by the barking of a dog. She had then thrown herself into a barbecue pit after a large party in New Mexico and had been rescued again—disfigured, but rescued. She had then, a month later, blown off a piece of her face with a sixteen-gauge shotgun, using a number nine shell. Rescued again, she had written two high-spirited and passionate letters to her uncle about her determination to die. These had inspired in Farragut a love for the blessed paradigm, the beauty of the establishment, the glory of organized society. Rachel was an aberration and Farragut would sweep her under the rug as her father seemed to have done. Eben's house, the cradle of these tragedies, was distinguished by its traditional composure.

The house was very old and so was most of the furniture. Eben had, quite unself-consciously, reconstructed the environment of what he claimed was his miserable youth. The blue china had been brought from Canton in a sailing ship by their great-grandfather and they had learned to crawl on the hieroglyphs woven into the Turkey rugs. Marcia and Zeke sat down and Eben went into the pantry to make some drinks. His wife, Carrie, was in the kitchen, sitting on a stool and crying.

"I'm leaving," she sobbed, "I'm leaving. I don't have to listen to your shit anymore."

"Oh, shut up," Eben shouted. "Shut up. Shut up. You've been leaving me weekly or oftener for as long as I can remember. You started leaving me before you asked me to marry you. My God! Unless you rent space in a warehouse, there isn't a place in the county with enough room for your clothes. You're about as portable as the Metropolitan Opera Company's production of *Turandot*. Just to get your crap out of here would keep the moving men busy for weeks. You have hundreds of dresses, hats, fur coats and shoes. I have to hang my clothes in the laundry. And then there's your piano and your grandfather's crappy library and that five-hundred-pound bust of Homer. . . ."

"I'm leaving," she sobbed, "I'm leaving."

"Oh, stop saying that," Eben shouted. "How can I be expected to take seriously, even in a quarrelsome way, a woman who relishes lying to herself?"

He closed the kitchen door and passed the drinks.

"Why are you so cruel?" Farragut asked.

"I'm not always cruel," he said.

"I think you are," said Marcia.

"I've gone to extraordinary lengths to build up some understanding," said Eben. "For example. Carrie wanted a television set for the kitchen and so I bought her an excellent set. The first thing in the morning she would go downstairs and start talking to the television. When she sleeps she wears a kind of hat like a shower cap and she puts a lot of rejuvenating oils on her face. So there she sits in the morning with this hat on, talking a mile a minute to the television set. She contradicts news reports, laughs at the jokes and keeps up a general conversation. When I go to work she doesn't say goodbye; she's too busy talking to the television. When I come home in the evening she sometimes says hello, but very seldom. She's usually too busy chatting with the newsmen to pay any attention to me. Then at half-past six she says, 'I'm putting your dinner on the table.' That's sometimes the only sentence I get out of her during a full day, sometimes a week, sometimes longer. Then she serves the food and takes her plate back to the kitchen and eats her dinner there, talking and laughing at a show called *Trial and Error*. When I go to bed she's talking to an old movie.

"So let me tell you what I did. I have a friend named Potter. He's a TV man. We ride into town on the train together sometimes. So I asked him if it was hard to get on *Trial and Error* and he said no, he thought he could arrange it. So he called me a few days later and said he thought they could use me on *Trial and Error* the next day. It's a live show and I was to get to the studio at five for makeup and so forth. It's one of those shows where you pay forfeits and what you had to do that night was to walk over a water tank on a tightrope. They gave me a suit of clothes because I'd get wet and I had to sign all sorts of releases. So I got into this suit and went through the first part of the show, smiling all the time at the cameras. I mean I was smiling at Carrie. I thought that for once she might be looking at my smile. Then I climbed up the ladder to the tightrope and started walking over the pool and fell in. The audience didn't laugh too uproariously so they taped in a lot of laughter. So then I got dressed and came home and shouted, 'Hey, hey, did you see me on television?' She was lying on a sofa in the living room by the big set. She was crying. So then I thought I'd done the wrong thing, that she was crying because I looked like such a fool, falling into the tank. She went on crying and sobbing and I said, 'What's the matter, dear?' and she said, 'They shot the mother polar bear, they shot the mother polar bear!' Wrong show. I got the wrong show, but you can't say that I didn't try."

When he got up to collect their glasses he moved the curtain at the window where he sat and Farragut saw that behind the curtain were two empty vodka bottles. That might account for his stolid, seafaring walk, his thick speech and his air of stupid composure. So with his wife sobbing in the kitchen and his poor daughter crazy and his son in jail, Farragut asked, "Eben, why do you live like this?"

"Because I love it," said Eben. Then he bent down, raised the old Turkey carpet and kissed it with his wet mouth.

"I know one thing," shouted Farragut. "I don't want to be your brother. I don't want anyone on the street, anywhere in the world, to say that I look like you. I'll be any kind of a freak or addict before I'll be mistaken for you. I'll do anything before I'll kiss a rug."

"Kiss my ass," said Eben.

"You've got Dad's great sense of humor," Farragut said.

"He wanted you to be killed," screamed Eben. "I bet you didn't know that. He loved me, but he wanted you to be killed. Mother told me. He had an abortionist come out to the house. Your own father wanted you to be killed."

Then Farragut struck his brother with a fire iron. The widow testified that Farragut had struck his brother eighteen to twenty times, but she was a liar, and Farragut thought the doctor who corroborated this lie contemptible.

The trial that followed was, he thought, a mediocre display of a decadent judiciary. He was convicted as a drug addict and a sexual adventurer and sentenced to jail for the murder of his brother. "Your sentence would be lighter were you a less fortunate man," said the judge, "but society has lavished and wasted her riches upon you and utterly failed to provoke in you that conscience that is the stamp of an educated and civilized human being and a useful member of society." Marcia had said nothing in his defense, although she had smiled at him when she was on the stand, smiled at him sadly while she agreed to their description of the grueling humiliation of being married to a drug addict who put the procurement of his fix miles ahead of his love for his wife and his only son. There were the stalenesses of the courthouse to remember, the classroom window shades, the sense of an acute tedium that was like the manipulations of the most pitiless and accomplished torturer, and if the last he would see of the world was the courthouse, he claimed he had no regrets, although he would, in fact, have clung to any floorboard, spittoon or worn bench if he thought that it might save him.

"I'm dying, Zeke, I'm dying," said Chicken Number Two. "I can feel that I'm dying, but it ain't done my brain no harm, it ain't done my brain no harm, it ain't done my brain no harm, it ain't done my brain no harm." He slept.

Farragut remained where he was. He heard music and voices from the radios and the TV. There was still some light in the window. Chicken Number Two woke suddenly and said, "You see, Zeke, I ain't afraid of dying at all. I know that sounds lying and when people used to say to me that because they had already tasted death they weren't afraid of death I figured they were talking with no class, no class at all. It seemed to me that you didn't have any quality when you talked like that, it was like thinking you looked beautiful in a mirror—this shit about being fearless before death ain't got no quality. How could you say you were fearless about leaving the party when it's like a party, even in stir—even franks and rice taste good when you're hungry, even an iron bar feels good to touch, it feels good to sleep. It's like a party even in maximum security and who wants to walk out of a party into something that nobody knows anything at all about? If you think like that you ain't got no class. But I feel I've been around longer than fifty-two years. I know you think I'm younger. Everybody does, but I'm really fifty-two. But take you, for instance. You ain't never done nothing for me. And then take the Cuckold, for instance. He's done everything for me. He gets me my smokes, my paper, my outside food and I get along with him fine, but I don't like him. What I'm trying to say is that I ain't learned all I know through experience. I ain't learned through experience at all. I like you and I don't like the Cuckold and it's that way all down the line and so I figure I must come into this life with the memories of some other life and so it stands that I'll be going into something else and you know what, Zeke, you know what, I can hardly wait to see what it's going to be like, I can hardly wait. I don't want to sound like one of those freaks who ain't got no class, one of those freaks who go around saying that since they have tasted death they got no fear, no fear at all. I got class. I mean like right now, right now if they were going to take me out before a firing squad I'd go out laughing—I don't mean bitter laughing or broken-hearted laughing, I mean real laughing. I'd go out there and I'd dance my soft-shoe and with luck I'd have a good hard-on and then when they got the command to fire I'd throw my arms out so as not to waste any of their ammunition, so as to get the full benefit of their banging, and then I'd go down a very happy man because I'm intensely interested in what's going to happen next, I'm very interested in what's going to happen next."

There was still a little light in the window. Dance music came from Ransome's radio and at the end of the corridor on TV he could see a group of people having trouble. An old man was intoxicated with the past. A young man was intoxicated with the future. There was a young woman who had trouble with her lovers and an old woman who could be seen hiding gin bottles in hatboxes, refrigerators and bureau drawers. Out of the window beyond their heads and shoulders Farragut could see waves breaking on a white beach and the streets of a village and the trees of a forest, but why did they all stay in one room, quarreling, when they could walk to the store or eat a picnic in the woods or go for a swim in the sea? They were free to do all of this. Why did they stay indoors? Why didn't they hear the sea calling to them as Farragut heard it calling, imagined the clearness of the brine as it fanned out over the beautiful pebbles? Chicken Number Two snored loudly or his breathing was guttural or perhaps this was the death rattle.

The instant seemed conspiratorial in its intensity. Farragut felt pursued but easily ahead of his pursuers. Cunning was needed; cunning he seemed to possess, that and tenderness. He went to the chair beside Chicken Number Two's bed and took the dying man's warm hand in his. He seemed to draw from Chicken Number Two's presence a deep sense of freeness; he seemed to take something that Chicken Number Two was lovingly giving to him. He felt some discomfort in the right cheek of his buttocks, and half-standing, he saw that he had been sitting on Chicken's false teeth. "Oh, Chicken," he cried, "you bit me in the ass." His laughter was the laughter of the deepest tenderness and then he began to sob. His sobbing was convulsive and he rode it and let it run its course. He then called Tiny. Tiny came without asking any questions. "I'll get a doctor," he said. Then, seeing Chicken's naked arm with its dense and faded designs of gray tattooing, he said, "I don't think he spent no two thousand on tattoos like he said. It looks more like two hundred to me. He strangled an old woman. She had eighty-two dollars in her sugar bowl." Then he left. The light in the window was gone. The dance music and the misunderstandings on TV went on and on.

When the doctor came in he wore the same hat he had worn when he gave them short arm during the revolution. He still seemed unclean. "Call heaven," he said to Tiny. "We can't move no stiffs until twenty-two hundred," said Tiny. "That's the law." "Well, call later, then. He won't ferment. He's nothing but bones." They left and then Veronica and one of the other nurses came in with a canoe-shaped form made of light metal, which contained a long tan sack. They put Chicken into this and went away. Both the TV and Ransome's radio were giving commercials and Ransome tuned up his radio, a kindness perhaps.

Farragut stood with difficulty. Cunning was needed; cunning and the courage to take his rightful place in things as he saw them. He unzipped the sack. The noise of the zipper was some plainsong—some matter-of-fact memory of closing suitcases, toilet kits and clothes bags before you went to catch the plane. Bending over the sack, his arms and shoulders readied for some weight, he found that Chicken Number Two weighed nothing at all. He put Chicken into his own bed and was about to climb into the burial sack when some chance, some luck, some memory led him to take a blade out of his razor before he lay down in the cerements and zipped them up over his face. It was very close in there, but the smell of his grave was no more than the plain smell of canvas; the smell of some tent.

The men who came to get him must have worn rubber soles because he didn't hear them come in and didn't know they were there until he felt himself being lifted up off the floor and carried. His breath had begun to wet the cloth of his shroud and his head had begun to ache. He opened his mouth very wide to breathe, afraid that they would hear the noise he made and more afraid that the stupid animalism of his carcass would panic and that he would convulse and yell and ask to be let out. Now the cloth was wet, the wetness strengthened the stink of rubber and his face was soaked and he was panting. Then the panic passed and he heard the opening and the closing of the first two gates and felt himself being carried down the slope of the tunnel. He had never, that he remembered, been carried before. (His long-dead mother must have carried him from place to place, but he could not remember this.) The sensation of being carried belonged to the past, since it gave him an unlikely feeling of innocence and purity. How strange to be carried so late in life and toward nothing that he truly knew, freed, it seemed, from his erotic crudeness, his facile scorn and his chagrined laugh—not a fact, but a chance, something like the afternoon light on high trees, quite useless and thrilling. How strange to be living and to be grown and to be carried.

He felt the ground level off at the base of the tunnel near the delivery entrance and heard the guard at post number 8 say, "Another Indian bit the dust. What do you do with No Known Relatives or Concerned?" "NKRC's get burned cheap," said one of the carriers. Farragut heard the last prison bars open and close and felt the uneven footing of the drive. "Don't drop him, for Christ's sake," said the first carrier. "For Christ's sake don't drop him." "Look at that fucking moon, will you?" said the second carrier. "Will you look at that fucking moon?" They would be passing the main entrance then and going toward the gate. He felt himself being put down. "Where's Charlie?" said the first carrier. "He said he'd be late," said the second. "His mother-in-law had a heart attack this morning. He's coming in his own car, but his wife had to take it to the hospital." "Well, where's the hearse?" said the first carrier. "In for a lube and an oil change," said the second. "Well, I'll be Goddamned," said the first. "Cool it, cool it," said the second. "You're getting time and a half for doing nothing. Last year, the year before, sometime before Peter bought the beauty parlor, Pete and me had to carry out a three-hundred-pounder. I always thought I could lift a hundred and fifty easy, but we had to rest about ten times to get that NKRC out of here. We were both puffing. You wait here. I'll go up to the main building and call Charlie and see where he is." "What kind of a car's he got?" asked the first. "A wagon," said the second. "I don't know what year. Secondhand, I guess. He put a new fender on himself. He's had trouble with the distributor. I'll call him." "Wait a minute, wait a minute," said the first. "You got a match?" "Yeah," said the second. "Your face and my ass." Farragut heard a match being struck. "Thanks," said the first, and he heard the footsteps of the second walk away.

He was outside the gate or anyhow near the gate. The watchtowers were unarmed at that hour, but there was the moon to worry about. His life hung on the light of the moon and a secondhand car. The distributor would fail, the carburetor would flood, and they would go off together looking for tools while Farragut escaped. Then he heard another voice: "You want a beer?" "You got one?" asked the carrier unenthusiastically, and Farragut heard them walk away.

By bracing his shoulders and his arms, he checked the stress points in his shroud. The warp of the canvas was reinforced with rubber. The neck or crown of the shroud was heavy wire. He got the razor blade out of his pocket and began to cut, parallel to the zipper. The blade penetrated the canvas, but slowly. He needed time, but he would not pray for time or pray for anything else. He would settle for the stamina of love, a presence he felt like the beginnings of some stair. The blade fell from his fingers onto his shirt and in a terrified and convulsive and clumsy lurch he let the blade slip into the sack. Then, groping for it wildly, he cut his fingers, his trousers and his thigh. Stroking his thigh, he could feel the wetness of the blood, but this seemed to have happened to someone else. With the wet blade between his fingers, he went on cutting away at his bonds. Once his knees were free he raised them, ducked his head and shoulders from under the crown and stepped out of his grave.

Clouds hid the light of the moon. In the windows of a watch house he could see two men. One of them drank from a can. Near where he had lain was a pile of stones, and trying to judge what his weight would be in stones, he put a man's weight into the shroud so that they would feed stones to the fire. He walked quite simply out of the gates into a nearby street that was narrow and where most of the people would be poor and where most of the houses were dark.

He put one foot in front of the other. That was about it. The streets were brightly lighted, for this was at that time in our history when you could read the small print in a prayerbook in any street where the poor lived. This scrupulous light was meant to rout rapists, muggers and men who would strangle old women of eighty-two. The strong light and the black shadow he threw did not alarm him, nor was he alarmed by the thought of pursuit and capture, but what did frighten him was the possibility that some hysteria of his brain might cripple his legs. He put one foot in front of the other. His foot was wet with blood, but he didn't care. He admired the uniform darkness of the houses. No lights burned at all—no lights of sickness, worry or love—not even those dim lights that burn for the sake of children or their sensible fears of the dark. Then he heard a piano. It could not, that late at night, have been a child, but the fingers seemed stiff and ungainly and so he guessed it was someone old. The music was some beginner's piece—some simple minuet or dirge read off a soiled, dog-eared piece of sheet music—but the player was someone who could read music in the dark since the house where the music came from was dark.

The wall of buildings gave way to two empty lots where the houses had been razed and seized upon as a dump in spite of the NO DUMPING and FOR SALE signs. He saw a three-legged washing machine and the husk of a car. His response to this was deep and intuitive, as if the dump were some reminder of his haunted country. He deeply inhaled the air of the dump although it was no more than the bitterness of an extinguished fire. Had he raised his head, he would have seen a good deal of velocity and confusion as the clouds hurried past the face of a nearly full moon, so chaotically and so swiftly that they might have reminded him, with his turn of mind, not of fleeing hordes but of advancing ranks and throngs, an army more swift than bellicose, a tardy regiment. But he saw nothing of what was going on in heaven because his fear of falling kept his eyes on the sidewalk, and anyhow there was nothing to be seen there that would be of any use.

Then way ahead of him and on the right he saw a rectangle of pure white light and he knew he had the strength to reach this though the blood in his boot now made a noise. It was a laundromat. Three men and two women of various ages and colors were waiting for their wash. The doors to most of the machines hung open like the doors to ovens. Opposite were the bull's-eye windows of drying machines and in two he could see clothes tossed and falling, always falling—falling heedlessly, it seemed, like falling souls or angels if their fall had ever been heedless. He stood at the window, this escaped and bloody convict, watching these strangers wait for their clothes to be clean. One of the women noticed him and came to the window to see him better, but his appearance didn't alarm her at all, he was pleased to see, and when she had made sure that he was not a friend, she turned to walk back to her machine.

At a distant corner under a street light he saw another man. This could be an agent from the Department of Correction, he guessed, or given his luck so far, an agent from heaven. Above the stranger was a sign that said: BUS STOP. NO PARKING. The stranger smelled of whiskey and at his feet was a suitcase draped with clothes on hangers, an electric heater with a golden bowl shaped like the sun and a sky-blue motorcycle helmet. The stranger was utterly inconsequential, beginning with his lanky hair, his piecemeal face, his spare, piecemeal frame and his highly fermented breath. "Hi," he said. "What you see here is a man who is been evicted. This ain't everything I own in the world. I'm making my third trip. I'm moving in with my sister until I find another place. You can't find nothing this late at night. I ain't been evicted because of non-payment of rent. Money I got. Money's one thing I don't have to worry about. I got plenty of money. I been evicted because I'm a human being, that's why. I make noises like a human being, I close doors, I cough sometimes in the night, I have friends in now and then, sometimes I sing, sometimes I whistle, sometimes I do yoga, and because I'm human and make a little noise, a little human noise going up and down the stairs, I'm being evicted. I'm a disturber of the peace."

"That's terrible," said Farragut.

"You hit the nail on the head," said the stranger, "you hit the nail on the head. My landlady is one of those smelly old widows—they're widows even when they got a husband drinking beer in the kitchen—one of those smelly old widows who can't stand life in any form, fashion or flavor. I'm being evicted because I'm alive and healthy. This ain't all I own, by a long shot. I took my TV over on the first trip. I got a beauty. It's four years old, color, but when I had a little snow and asked the repairman to come in, he told me never, never turn this set in for a new one. They don't make them like this anymore, he said. He got rid of the snow and all he charged me was two dollars. He said it was a pleasure to work on a set like mine. It's over to my sister's now. Christ, I hate my sister and she hates my guts, but I'll spend the night there and find a beautiful place in the morning. They have some beautiful places on the south side, places with views of the river. You wouldn't want to share a place with me, would you, if I found something beautiful?"

"Maybe," said Farragut.

"Well, here's my card. Call me if you feel like it. I like your looks. I can tell you got a nice sense of humor. I'm in from ten to four. I sometimes come in a little later, but I don't go out for lunch. Don't call me at my sister's. She hates my guts. Here's our bus."

The brightly lighted bus had the same kind and number of people—for all he knew, the same people—

that he had seen in the laundromat. Farragut picked up the heater and the motorcycle helmet and the stranger went ahead of him with his suitcase and his clothes. "Be my guest," he said over his shoulder, paying Farragut's fare. He took the third seat on the left, by the window, and said to Farragut, "Sit here, sit down here." Farragut did. "You meet all kinds, don't you?" he went on. "Imagine calling me a disorderly person just because I sing and whistle and make a little noise going up and down the stairs at night. Imagine. Hey, it's raining," he exclaimed, pointing to the white streaks on the window. "Hey, it's raining and you ain't got no coat. But I got a coat here, I got a coat here I think'll fit you. Wait a minute." He pulled a coat out of the clothes. "Here, try this on."

"You'll need your coat," Farragut said.

"No, no, try it on. I got three raincoats. Moving around from place to place all the time, I don't lose stuff, I accumulate stuff, like I already got a raincoat at my sister's and a raincoat in the lost and found room at the Exeter House and this one I got on. And this one. That makes four. Try it on."

Farragut put his arms into the sleeves and settled the coat around his shoulders. "Perfect, perfect," exclaimed the stranger. "It's a perfect fit. You know, you look like a million dollars in that coat. You look like you just deposited a million dollars in the bank and was walking out of the bank, very slowly, you know, like you was going to meet some broad in a very expensive restaurant and buy her lunch. It's a perfect fit."

"Thank you very much," said Farragut. He stood

and shook the stranger's hand. "I'm getting off at the
next stop."

"Well, that's all right," said the stranger. "You got
my telephone number. I'm in from ten to four, maybe
a little later. I don't go out for lunch, but don't call me
at my sister's."

Farragut walked to the front of the bus and got off
at the next stop. Stepping from the bus onto the street,
he saw that he had lost his fear of falling and all other
fears of that nature. He held his head high, his back
straight, and walked along nicely. Rejoice, he thought,
rejoice.

The text of this book was set on the Linotype in a new face called Primer, designed by Rudolph Ruzicka, who was earlier responsible for the design of Fairfield and Fairfield Medium, Linotype faces whose virtues have for some time been accorded wide recognition.

The complete range of sizes of Primer was first made available in 1954, although the pilot size of 12-point was ready as early as 1951. The design of the face makes general reference to Linotype Century—long a serviceable type, totally lacking in manner or frills of any kind—but brilliantly corrects its characterless quality.

The book was composed, printed and bound by American Book–Stratford Press, Inc., Saddle Brook, New Jersey.

Typography and binding design by Camilla Filancia.